MURDER AT ABBEY HEAD

An addictive crime mystery full of twists

ROY LEWIS

Arnold Landon Mysteries Book 17

Originally published as
The Ways of Death

Revised edition 2022
Joffe Books, London
www.joffebooks.com

First published in Great Britain in 2002
as *The Ways of Death*

This paperback edition was first published
in Great Britain in 2022

ISBN: 978-1-80405-326-3

NOTE TO THE READER

Please note this book is set in the early 2000s in England, a time before ubiquitous CCTV, and when social attitudes were very different.

There is a way which seemeth right unto a man but the end thereof are the ways of death.

Proverbs 14:12

PROLOGUE

From the beginning, it had been a sacred place.

Offshore lay the islands, golden in the sun, and in the ancient time of the dreaming the shamans had drawn their song lines, marking their mythic, drug-induced journeys on the smooth-faced rock, high on the wide sweep of the headland above the crashing sea. As the millennia had passed the islands had disappeared and the headland had grown, its flanks stark and gaunt under the carving, keening east wind from the sea, but on the rock face itself depictions of trance dances were still etched and drawn. Distorted human shapes, abstract entoptic imagery, fine patterned petroglyphs that identified the cults that had grown and waned over the centuries.

The carvings were sources of power, emphasizing the dissonance between man's view of the physical world he inhabited and the terrible power of the spirit territory. The rain-bull was captured there, a complex metaphor in the weather-magic of the shamans. The rock was the interface between one world and another, darker habitation, and they marked the rock with depictions of hybrid spirits, man-animal figures emerging from the cracks and crevices of the cliff face, to disappear, snake-tailed into other, deeper fissures.

Later, when the day of the sunwatcher priests came to the headland, the influence of potent hallucinogens converted out-of-body experiences into depictions of flying men, rock spirits, geometric carvings that lived for centuries before the wild rain and wind and the invading sea tore and scratched and scraped at them till only scattered engravings high on the indented cliff remained to mark the transient passage of men's beliefs.

And the world turned, and the heavens watched the millennia pass until the supernova burst in the skies, the moon visible as a crescent near the exploding star. It created a new vision in the minds of men, reflected by starbursts painted on the rock, stations on the old, invisible, mythic routes that men trod in the collective knowledge of their dreams, mapping the minds of the shaman-priests, sinking back into the land as generations passed, re-emerging again as half-forgotten beliefs and memories.

The ebb and flow of the sea, retreating and invading as successive ice-ages came and went, changed the nature of the sight-lines from the clifftop but it remained a magic place. The islands had gone, ancient settlements on the flood plain below had been washed away, men had lived and died on the cliff, were buried and resurrected, and at one time their ritual footprints had been carved in the living rock — dead men walking. Dead men, and spirits, shadows on the sea. Beliefs and traditions came and went, and shamans sang their soul songs, but one place never changed in the riveting grasp it maintained on men's imaginations.

The deep cleft in the flat bare rock of the headland had been torn by a lightning bolt that had severed the ground in a jagged, convoluted wound of bubbling rock. The depth of the opening was unknown, the pit fissuring down into the heart of the cliff, its blackness unplumbed. Its vulvic appearance however engaged the minds of men who identified it as the physical entrance to the chthonic spirit world, the abode of the earth mother: into its echoing depths were cast votive offerings, artefacts, bear skulls, animals — and men. In the

2

womb-like sea caves below, carved relentlessly out of the foot of the cliff, rituals that had been held for centuries could be wiped out in a moment as the sea returned, thundering inwards to reclaim lost territory, or as the tired rock collapsed under the ceaseless beat of rain and wind, driving in from the menacing east. But on the clifftop, the deep, mysterious cleft remained. It seemed to harbour a female energy that called out to the spirits, and provided a birthplace for the imaginations of men.

And it spoke to them.

The sound was unlike anything they had heard in the physical world. When the skies were dark it could be a keening sound, weeping for lost souls and broken promises. It was a deep rumbling of anger, fury at the fickleness of human beliefs. It was the satisfied growling of an appeased spirit or the lulling whisper of sexual secrets; and it could be the screaming pain of a birth and a predicted death.

So in their terror men worshipped at the vulvic shrine of the clefted rock, cast their offerings into it, prayed to its gaping, corrugated, lobed mouth, and sought appeasement, and good fortune in war, and fine harvests, good winters. And in response it talked to the shamans, communicated with the priests, murmured and replied to those who would listen, and always it remained, gaping, breathing spasmodically to the sky as generations of men's lives came, and passed, until the Old Ones had gone and new visions came to the land.

CHAPTER ONE

1

Arnold Landon was never quite sure whether he preferred things when Karen Stannard was away from the office at the Department of Museums and Antiquities or not. There was no doubt her presence tended to sharpen expectations in the department. The shivering tension was the result of the combination of her incredible beauty, undoubted intelligence, unrelenting perfectionism, and occasional unpredictability. There was an electricity in the air when she was around, though the pressure on her colleagues had eased somewhat now that she was secure in her position as head of department. She no longer felt it necessary to be always searching for perceived slights and power challenges. Even so, the mere fact she was in the building could result in a subtle change in the atmosphere.

'Let's face it,' Portia Tyrrel had once said to Arnold mocking him with her wise eyes, 'she's got you men exactly where she wants you. Little boys, standing on one foot, smutty thoughts in your minds but ready to jump at the voice of authority.'

And she had a point, Arnold considered. Karen Stannard's beauty might make a man think of things other than archaeology, but her tone could cut him down to size. And she was very careful of her status and position. There were certain tasks she would never delegate. She had made that clear to Arnold — whom she had always, erroneously, regarded as a rival — when she had advised him that the Chief Executive's committee had agreed to his appointment as her deputy. 'I expect loyalty from you, of course,' she had said quietly, smiling at him, swivelling in her chair to cross one provocative, sheer-sheathed leg over the other. 'But there are limits, boundaries to be drawn and observed religiously. I will be detailing certain activities into your hands — I shan't be breathing over your shoulder, watching your every move. We've worked together now for a few years, and I know I can trust you.'

The slight self-mockery in her eyes told him she knew, as he did, that the words were not strictly true.

'So I won't be harassing you over the standard things,' she went on, 'but I will expect you to report to me on all the important issues that might arise from time to time. *Before* you actually take action on them. For the protection of the department, of course,' she added sweetly, but meaning herself. 'And in my absence, which will be inevitable from time to time, you will act with my full authority, naturally.'

There had been a slight pause at that point. The colour of her eyes had seemed to change in dark reflection, and Arnold guessed that she still had reservations on the matter, which Chief Executive Powell Frinton, aware of the latent tensions between the two of them, would have insisted upon. 'But I know you have the good sense,' she continued, 'to behave in no way that might cause . . . difficulties to arise for me when I return.' She had given him a heart-warming, seductive smile, one close friend knifing another. 'After all, we must work together, mustn't we?'

And Arnold's duties in taking responsibility for the department had arisen sooner than he had expected — only days after her confirmed appointment, in fact. Karen had called him into her office, to explain.

'I shall be in London for a week,' she announced brusquely. 'I shall be part of the delegation from the council, and there will be meetings held at the ministry in Whitehall, and then with the Heritage people. Things have got serious.'

'In what respect?'

Her long, slim fingers had tapped the file in front of her as she frowned. 'You'll have seen the recent press reports — and it's been on television as well. They had a programme on the BBC the other evening, highlighting the issue. *Landslip!* they called it. Dramatic.'

'The scenes shown were dramatic enough,' Arnold said mildly. 'The sea defences along the north-east coast have certainly taken a pounding this winter. Erosion of the limestone cliffs, loss of five fishermen cottages at Roundsay Bay, that hotel threatened on the headland — the coastline certainly seems to have taken a beating.'

'Yes, yes,' she said impatiently, 'I saw the programme. Anyway, the council will be using some of that footage to strengthen their case for grant support to rebuild some of the sea walls, shore up the staithes, and reconstruct two of the harbour sites.'

'Which is where we come in?'

Karen Stannard nodded. She raised an elegant eyebrow, observing him thoughtfully, her head tilted slightly so that the morning sun streaming in through the window caught stray glints of gold in her hair. 'There'll be a dredging operation before they can rebuild the harbour walls, and we'll need a team up there at Roundsay and at the Devil's Hole.'

'To look for evidence of Roman occupation at Roundsay,' Arnold nodded, 'and at the Devil's Hole . . . ?'

She sighed. 'The councillors want us to look for anything that will support the tourist industry — you know, did the name come from Viking incursions, or local wrecking activities — or both. Anyway, I want you to take charge of both those teams. Then there's the matter of the sea cave at Abbey Head. I thought maybe Portia . . .' She watched his reaction carefully for a moment, calculating. Arnold felt slightly uncomfortable, he knew she had suspicions about his relationship with her half-Singaporean assistant. He was disinclined to satisfy her curiosity. 'Anyway,' she went on after a moment, 'if there's anything else that comes up short term, you can deal with it. There shouldn't be anything important. And I'll be back in a week. You can give me a full report then . . .'

In the event, there was not a great deal to report, he concluded as the week drew to its close. Other than the matter of Sylvie Hayman's suicide.

* * *

Chris Hayman had worked in the Department of Museums and Antiquities even longer than Arnold had. He had already been on the staff when Arnold had transferred from the Planning Department. They had never had much to do with each other. Hayman had occasionally assisted at some of the digs, but had spent most of his time of recent years buried in the archival section, filing, cataloguing, and latterly transferring old records to computer files. His name was rarely mentioned among the staff. He seemed to have made no close friends in the department at all in spite of the length of time he had worked there. He was in his fifties now, a stocky, close-mouthed, solitary kind of man who kept his own counsel, allowed no colleagues to get to know him well, maintained a life private to himself outside work. And it would have remained so, if his wife had not died.

It would normally have been a task that Karen Stannard would have undertaken as head of department, attending the funeral of Chris Hayman's wife, but Arnold suspected she might in any event have tried to delegate it to him. As it was, she was in London, a departmental presence was necessary as a mark of respect, and so it was Arnold who had to put in the appearance. A mark of respect, support for a colleague at a difficult time, even for a man who had kept so much to himself over the years.

But when Arnold arrived at the small church at Abbey village he was somewhat unnerved to find that not only was he the only person to have come from the department, but there were no more than three people, apart from Chris Hayman and the vicar, in the church itself.

The echoes in the cold vaulted building seemed to emphasize that Sylvie Hayman had slipped out of the world almost unnoticed. While the organ was badly played by a shiny-suited, skeletal man who shook with a palsied twitch at intervals, Arnold allowed his thoughts to stray at first to observing the structure of the church itself. It was unproductive. Whatever had been its origins, and in Arnold's experience most village churches could lay claim to extensive histories, the story that might have been told by its stones had been buried under swathes of Victorian reconstructions, driven more by religious fervour than common sense. Stark pews, bare walls, crudely renewed stained glass . . . His attention wandered to the two old ladies huddled near the bier. Like the bald old man at the other side of the aisle, they would be habitues of funerals, planning their own entry into Paradise, perhaps cackling later at the manner in which they were still cheating the Reaper, nursing their ages with stubborn pride, checking the local newspaper for signs of each other's obituaries.

Arnold's attention wandered back to Chris Hayman. He sat upright in the pew, near the bier. He still had a good, strong head of hair: dark, greying at the temples, cut short, aggressively. Arnold had met him from time to time in the canteen: a stocky, hard-bodied man with an air of suppressed belligerence, an intelligent man, Arnold guessed, with a strong prow of a nose, and hard eyes. There were some who suggested he had an attitude problem, seeming to regard the world as hostile, and that was why he had never risen in the department over the years. Others suggested it was because he had never been interested in promotion, had kept to himself, had lived his own enclosed life the way he had wanted it. No children, apparently; no family. No interests that anyone in the department was aware of.

The death of his wife would have hit him hard, Arnold guessed.

He wondered whether Hayman had met with any opposition when the matter of the funeral had come up. A suicide, being buried in consecrated ground. Some vicars could be difficult. This one, a thin, frail man who shuddered at the graveside under the cutting wind that tugged at his vestments, would probably have been unable to resist pressure from an insistent Chris Hayman. The bereaved man stood impassively, eyes lowered, black-coated, black-gloved hands clasped in front of him as the body of his wife was lowered into the grave. One of the women present gave a strange clucking sound. The vicar intoned meaningless words that were snatched away by the wind. They all turned away, eventually, shuffling out of the churchyard to leave the final work to others. They were standing a little distance away, two men leaning on shovels.

Arnold walked slowly down the narrow path between leaning headstones, and stopped near the fifteenth-century lychgate. He waited as Chris Hayman approached. The man looked up, expressionlessly; there seemed to be no glint of recognition in his eyes. He would have stepped past if Arnold had not spoken.

'I didn't have a chance of a word earlier,' Arnold said awkwardly. 'But I'd like to express my condolences now.'

Chris Hayman stopped abruptly, raised his head, as though sniffing the wind, seeking threats of rain in the grey skies. He nodded. 'Right weather for it, anyway. Bloody depressing.'

Arnold felt uneasy, not knowing what to say. 'Miss Stannard would have come, of course, but she's away at the moment. So I'm here to . . . to represent the department.'

'Duty.' Chris Hayman nodded, understanding. He glanced around him, watched the shuffling women heading home. 'Don't know who they were. Regulars, I suppose.'

'Not neighbours?' Arnold asked.

Hayman shook his head. 'No, we . . . I don't live here in Abbey village. Just that it's the nearest church, you know. Don't even know anyone in the village. No need.' He frowned, reflectively. 'Same with the department, really. Do your job, get on with your life, don't know many people. No need.'

Arnold looked about him, awkwardly. 'Well, I'm sure there would have been others here from the department, but the way things are at the moment, the pressures we're under—'

'No,' Hayman contradicted him flatly. 'It's all right. I expected no one.' Dark eyes, hooded under heavy black eyebrows, fixed curiously on Arnold. 'I'm surprised to see you, in fact. I understand it was duty . . . but even so. It wasn't necessary.' He grunted, shoved his gloved hands into the pockets of his black knee-length woollen coat. 'There's a tradition up here in the north-east, of course.'

'Tradition?'

'Wake. Like the Irish. And the Welsh, I'm led to believe. Come to the church, attend the graveside. Then, like in repayment, go back to the house. Ham sandwiches. Cup of tea. Later, get out the whisky. Sit around, gossip, tell stories about the deceased. Lot of laughter, I understand. Merriment. Relief of tension. Merriment, and funny stories . . . but what if there's none to tell?'

Arnold shuffled, wishing he was elsewhere.

'Anyway,' Hayman continued gruffly. 'No wake. Didn't expect anyone. No wake! No stories, no entertainment.' He eyed Arnold sourly. 'But you took the trouble to come, so the least I can do is offer you a drink. There's a pub down in the village.'

'I'm not sure . . .' Arnold replied doubtfully.

'Don't be so bloody prissy,' Hayman said and marched off towards the village. Somewhat reluctantly Arnold followed him.

* * *

Abbey village consisted of a huddle of cottages, some eighteenth-century in construction, leading into a main street containing one general store and a pub called the Black Horse. At the far end of the street Arnold could see the beginning of a small estate of modern bungalows and terraced houses, built for overspill families from Newcastle, people who were unwanted, unwelcome and destructive of the old village atmosphere. Just beyond the housing estate, providentially, there was a police training school, housed on premises which were formerly used by a college specializing in agricultural education. Its location meant that a controlling and sobering influence was felt in the area, not least in the prevailing circumstances under which, Arnold had heard, undesirable influences were being relocated to Abbey. He could understand why Chris Hayman would not be interested in living in the village, or in getting to know people living there. There was a transient air to the huddle of houses, in spite of their age. It was as though, like the old ladies in the church, they were waiting to move on to better things.

The Black Horse was comfortable enough, Arnold concluded: unpretentious, scarred wooden tables, elderly upholstered chairs, a threadbare carpet and a brass foot rail at the bar — because of its location the pub had been spared the plastic garishness of brewery modernization. It was surprisingly busy: there was a team of men playing competitive darts in the far corner beyond the bar, a small room to one side housed others engaged in bar billiards, and under the window was a tight group of men, huddled together at their table, heads together, murmuring almost conspiratorially.

As Arnold and Hayman entered the room and made their way towards the bar there was a sudden hush. Arnold looked around and people seemed to be staring at them expectantly: the man holding the darts had paused, activity had ceased in the billiard room, heads had turned at the conspiratorial table and everything seemed to have stopped, time and activity suspended, as though they were all waiting for something to happen.

Hayman seemed oblivious to the atmosphere, but Arnold sensed an almost electric tension in the room. At the conspiratorial table he caught a glimpse of a thickset man in a heavy polo-necked sweater, raising his head in appraisal, staring aggressively at him. He had grey, short-cropped hair, burly shoulders hunched in tightly suppressed eagerness, a coiled spring waiting for release. Their glances locked and Arnold sensed some inexplicable challenge directed against him. Then the moment was broken as something was said, a burst of laughter came from a group of young men at the far end of the room dressed in dark blue jerseys, smartly turned out, clean-shaven, scrubbed, pints of beer in front of them, laughing, joking, chatting. Police cadets, Arnold guessed, or maybe young serving officers on a course.

The man in the polo-necked sweater looked away, relaxed visibly. The darts players returned to their game. There was the clink of cue on billiard ball and Chris Hayman leaned on the bar and ordered two large whiskies, without reference to Arnold's wishes. When the taciturn barman placed the drinks in front of Hayman he downed his in two quick gulps, then ordered another for himself. Arnold felt uneasy. He sipped at his whisky, glanced around the bar. Their presence was now being ignored. 'So is this your local?'

'Don't have a local,' Hayman grunted. 'I told you — this isn't my village. I got a place about two miles from here. Old gamekeeper's cottage, I would guess. Been there thirty years.' He was silent for a little while, eyeing his glass. 'She always hated it.'

'Your wife?'

He nodded. 'Sylvie always hated it. She used to say, every winter, she couldn't stand the whining noise of the wind in the chimney. I used to tell her it was in her head.'

'You never thought of moving elsewhere?' Arnold enquired.

'What for?' Hayman demanded, almost belligerently. 'It would have been the same anywhere else. I had my job in Morpeth, in the department. It gave us enough to live on, quietly. She worked for a while in one of the stores in town. But she didn't like it; gave it up eventually. Just stayed home.

Brooding. Churning over things that couldn't be changed. Listening to the wind in the chimney.' He swallowed his drink, glanced at Arnold's half-empty glass.

'Let me get you one,' Arnold suggested.

Hayman shook his leonine head. 'At a wake, the host pays.' He called to the barman, ordered two more drinks. Arnold felt ill at ease. The speed at which Hayman was drinking was alarming. It suggested he was out to get drunk, deliberately, perhaps as a shield against emotion.

'How long was your wife in a state of depression?' Arnold asked.

'How long?' Hayman snorted derisively. 'Thirty bloody years, I'd say. It was like a shawl she drew around her, to that extent, the cottage was the best place for her to live. She didn't need to be bothered with people. She could just stay there all day until I got home; by herself with just her pills for company.'

'She suffered from illness?'

Hayman shook his head. 'Only in her mind. You see . ..' He hesitated, as though reluctant to speak of things that had been held back, personal things he had failed to talk about in decades. 'Things could have been different. She . . . had expectations. No, that's not right. When I came to the north, when I met her she already had a good life, a solid background. You know she rode horses as a child? Big house, paddock . . . Parents who loved her, had money. Sylvie had been *comfortable*, you know what I mean? No worries about the future. And then we married, and everything changed.'

Arnold hesitated. He was in danger of trespassing in a time of personal grief, and yet there was something odd about Hayman. It seemed he wanted to talk, but his words carried no undertones of grief — rather, they were sustained by a subdued sense of outrage.

'There were times when I thought that maybe she blamed me for what happened,' Hayman muttered, with a surly edge to his tone. 'Times when she raged at me as though it was all my fault. But it had nothing to do with me. It was all about her father. He was a weak man. He had it all in his grasp, a good future to hand on to his daughter. And he blew it all away. Allowed himself to be cheated.' Hayman laughed suddenly, a mirthless sound as he held up his whisky glass. 'Blew it on the gaming tables, and drank himself into oblivion. Which is what I'm doing really right now. Isn't that so, Landon?'

'You ought to take it easy,' Arnold suggested quietly. 'I can understand—'

'How the hell can you possibly understand?' Hayman demanded aggressively. 'How the hell can you know what it was like?'

'I—'

A voice called out from across the room. It was the man in the polo-necked jersey. He was gesturing towards the doorway. Arnold glanced back and saw three men entering the bar. They were of a kind: shabbily dressed in worn jackets, stained jeans and heavy boots. The man who led them was advancing to the bar, with an air of grim purpose: his hair was dark and shaggy, his chin black-stubbled. His companions were shorter than he, stocky, heavy-shouldered and less certain of themselves, as though they entered the bar with a degree of trepidation. The last one, the youngest, glanced around nervously. The man with the short-cropped hair was staring at them with unveiled animosity. Suddenly, the tension was back in the room, and the expectant hush had returned.

'How can you possibly know what it was like?' Hayman continued, turning away, apparently indifferent to the change in the atmosphere. 'Her old man — Joe Angell — he had a good business, with bright prospects for growth. But he was a drunk and in a matter of years he'd killed himself. And when he was dead it all came crashing down. The house was gone, the paddock . . . there was no money, he'd been cheated out of the business. It was all gone. Then there was her mother. She couldn't handle the situation and in a way Sylvie was like her. After her mother died, there was only me, and that wasn't enough for Sylvie. She brooded, she couldn't let go of the past and how it should all have been different. She sank into depression. Can you imagine, Landon? Thirty years? Of course you can't.'

Arnold shuddered inwardly. He was beginning to understand what had shaped Chris Hayman's behaviour. A wife sunk into a depression that never changed; a cottage where the two of them would live out a married life that held no spark; for Hayman a retreat into a sullen locking out of friendships as with his wife he contemplated what could, what should have been.

'I always knew she'd do it in the end,' Hayman muttered bitterly. 'She threatened to, often enough — and there were more than enough bloody pills in the house. Like an apothecary's, it was.'

It was a strange word to use, Arnold thought. Apothecary. Before he could dwell too long on the matter however, the man with the short-cropped hair at the far end of the room shouted something. Arnold did not catch the words, but the tone was aggressive, jeering and insulting. The burly, leather-jacketed man standing beside them at the bar stiffened, but made no move to turn around. His companions shuffled uneasily. But the effect on Hayman was electric.

He turned his head, stared across the room at the man who had shouted. The heavyset man glared back belligerently, his grey cropped hair seeming to bristle, his eyes angry.

Then Chris Hayman turned back, looked at the man hunched beside him. He stared at him for several seconds, until at last, reluctantly, the man turned his own head. They locked glances for a long moment, the other man looked away and then Hayman growled something in a surly, spitting tone. The big man turned his head, and there was a stain of anger in his eyes. He glared at Hayman; his companions seemed suddenly edgy, the young man tugged at the sleeve of his leather jacket, but he dragged himself free, turned to face Hayman. The tension was alive in the room, an electric crackling in the air as the man across the room shouted again, jeering. The man in the leather jacket ignored the cat-calls but said something to Hayman in a language incomprehensible to Arnold. Next moment all hell broke loose.

To Arnold's amazement Hayman exploded into sudden violence. He shouted a curse at the big man and with a wild sweep of his arm hit him with his elbow, across the bridge of his nose. There was a cracking noise, the man in the leather jacket staggered back, collided with his companions, and then next moment, howling with rage, came charging back at Chris Hayman. There was uproar all around them. The man with the short-cropped hair was up from his table, charging across the room, and his companions were up with him. Hayman and his assailant were locked arm in arm, battering at each other, but at first it was an ineffective, aimless flailing that was achieving little. Blood from the big man's nose flew in a spray around them, but the man's companions were also now involved, and as the barman yelled for order the darts players came rushing across the room, whooping, joining in the fracas.

To Arnold's surprise they seemed intent on taking part in the battle rather than prising apart the two men who had started it. Tables were overturned, an atavistic howling arose, the sound of men releasing their tensions in an outburst of senseless violence. It was as though it had all been planned, old scores were being paid off, and the three men who had entered the bar were at the centre of the storm. Arnold plunged in, grabbing at Chris Hayman's arm, trying to pull him away. Hayman slipped, scrabbling to the floor, and Arnold could see his features were contorted with a crazy, uncontrollable rage. Arnold dragged at him, pulling him away as the fight extended, raging around them, and suddenly enveloping them.

Arnold found himself trapped in the thick of the swirling battle. Bodies swayed and struggled around him, a fist struck the side of his head and his senses whirled. He found himself fighting back, striking out, pushing, shoving as the levels of noise rose above them, and he caught a vague glimpse of the group of police cadets from the far end of the room rushing forward, piling into the scrum of struggling, shouting, beating bodies.

A boot struck him in the groin. He went down on one knee as pain surged like a knife through his lower body. He had lost his grip on Hayman, the yelling assault swirled around him, someone fell on him and he could smell acrid sweat mingled with the odours of fear and rage. An elbow took him in the right eye and his senses swam. He fell, another man's body heavy on his, and he was unable to move as boots stamped around him, bodies swayed above him and gradually he realized that the room was fading about him. He caught a glimpse of the man with short-cropped hair and wild, enraged eyes standing over him, kicking and fighting, fists bunched, arms whirling like a madman. Then there was a rush of bodies, a collapse of the group, and everything swirled into darkness and he could hear no more.

2

Detective Chief Inspector Culpeper raised his glass in salute to his old friend. 'So here's to a happy and lengthy retirement, Mac. What'll it be? Gardening? Walking? Propping up the bar at the local pub?'

'The last, most likely. Not like you. When your time comes, it'll be up to Seahouses, I suppose, messing about in boats. And it's not all that long to go now, is it?'

'Matter of weeks, I suppose,' Culpeper replied. 'And with luck, they'll be a quiet few weeks. I didn't end up with a cushy number like yours.'

'Aye,' Chief Inspector Macardle sighed in some satisfaction. 'I got to admit, it came pretty good for me in the end. I mean, can you imagine a berth out here in the countryside, young whippersnappers to chase around, coppers wet behind their ears and having to listen to everything I tell them. Training . . . not a bad way to finish up, I admit.'

Culpeper nodded, and strolled across to the window. The training centre comprised a series of long, low buildings — lecture rooms, sports centre, canteen, single bedroom accommodation — surrounded by several acres of land, set out to lawns mainly now, though previously it had served as a farm training college. He wasn't certain whether he envied

Macardle or not: there was something to be said for being given the opportunity to get off the streets, get away from the desk at HQ, and undertake the mundane activities of an administrator of a police training centre. On the other hand, Culpeper suspected, it wouldn't really have suited him, whatever he'd said to Macardle. He didn't think he could have happily spent his last few years as a copper doing other than he was presently detailed to do: chasing villains. It was what he had spent the last twenty years doing, and he was an old dog. New tricks weren't easy to take.

An old dog, with a spreading waistline, he sighed, catching a glimpse of his reflection in the window. A thick waist, grey-stubbled hair, and an attitude that the younger officers regarded as dinosaurian.

As if reading his mind, Macardle suddenly said, 'And how's young Farnsby?'

Culpeper gave a mock groan. 'Keen, perceptive, quick and a pain in the arse.'

Macardle chuckled. 'So nothing's changed?'

'Ha, he's all right, I suppose,' Culpeper conceded reluctantly. 'But he didn't come up the way we did, Mac, and it shows from time to time. Impatience, refusal to take advice, more than happy to go off on courses . . . he's just not put in the *street* time, you know what I mean?'

'And when you go?'

Culpeper turned away from the window and sipped at his drink. Talk of his own retirement always left him with a faintly uneasy, queasy feeling. It was not that he was reluctant to go, and he had plans for using his leisure time in retirement. It was just a vague feeling of anxiety, probably based on the fact that he knew it would be a sea-change for him. And for his wife. She was already moaning that she wouldn't want him under her feet in the house. 'When I go?' He shrugged. 'I'm pretty sure Farnsby will be expecting promotion. And these last few years I've had the impression that he's very much in favour with the top brass. But I don't know . . .'

He looked around the crowded room, thronged with eager-eyed, scrubbed young men, broad-shouldered, not entirely at ease in a party of this kind because there were too many senior officers present, but enjoying themselves well enough with the free booze available at Macardle's retirement celebration. 'I wonder where some of these will end up.'

Macardle smiled, and cast an indulgent, almost fatherly glance around the room. 'They're not high-flyers, that's for sure. But they're not bad lads, though I wouldn't tell them so. A few bright sparks. A few thugs, too. Same old mix, like in the old days. Nothing really changes.'

Culpeper nodded. 'I guess so. You and I, we put the boot in ourselves a few times, in the old Shields days, and along the Tyne back alleys.' His eyes gleamed as he looked around him. He gestured towards one group of young men, drinking near the bar. 'And as you say, nothing changes. They're carrying a few bruises. Looks like they been in the wars. And not on the rugby field either.'

Macardle nodded ponderously. 'Aye, they have that. They were up at a pub at Abbey village earlier today: it's their day off. They got more excitement than they'd expected. But they're good lads. One rang in; the others piled in, sorted out the trouble. But got their bruises to show for it.'

'So what was it all about?' Culpeper asked curiously. Macardle puffed out plump, reddened cheeks in exasperation. 'It's this bloody government dispersal policy, isn't it?'

'How do you mean?'

'They're flooding in at the Channel ports, as we know,' Macardle explained. 'Kosovans, Chinese, Turks, Iraqis, gipsies, Saudis, Romanians, Croatians, Moroccans, you name it, they're there. Riding the lorries, hiding in car boots, clinging to trains, stowing away aboard ferries. Some idiots have even hidden in aircraft undercarriages. Seeking the promised land, can you believe it? All claiming asylum, all seeking handouts, all wanting to work — they say — but once they've got into the system, they fade away into the black economy. And the towns down south, in Kent particularly, they've got fed up.

Huge backlog of immigration appeals, and these people have to be looked after somewhere. So the government's been trying to disperse them, so they don't have these ghettos arising in the south coast towns. Trouble is, these people don't want to disperse.'

'I heard there's some reluctance to come north,' Culpeper agreed.

'Damn right there is. Once they get bussed up here, half of them take one look at the lack of opportunities, turn round, hightail it back south and just disappear.' Macardle snorted in disgust. 'The local gangs have begun to sniff at it too. Never mind the snakeheads and the Triads: there's more than a few local villains here along the Tyne and Wear who've realized that smuggling people into the UK is even more profitable than smuggling cheap fags and booze. And the red light business has changed too, as a result. The prostitutes these days are rarely likely to be able to speak good English, I hear.'

'The punters aren't after good conversation though, are they?' Culpeper grinned. 'So was it immigrants that these lads of yours came up against today?'

'Not exactly.' Macardle wrinkled his nose. 'Not an organized gang. It's just that the powers that be decided, some time ago, that it would make sense to disperse some of these immigrants up to Northumberland, pending the hearing of their appeals against return to the Continent. I think it was a crazy decision — I mean, they find a quiet village, they create housing estates for overspill from Newcastle, they uproot people from the Tyne and expect them to settle in the countryside — when half of them were from families of street villains going back three generations at least — and then they add to the mix by shoving European immigrants right in the middle of them. The first dispersal was bad enough. Shoving foreigners into the situation was a recipe for trouble. Explosive.'

'And there's been trouble.'

Macardle ducked his head in agreement, finished his drink and scowled at his empty glass. 'You can say that again.

More than enough. It's not a large group, twenty or thirty East Europeans, Croats, Serbs, I don't know what the hell they are really. But there's an enclave of them at Abbey village, and the locals don't like it — they reckon chickens go missing, milk bottles disappear from doorsteps, incidents of burglary and thieving have increased — that sort of petty thing for God's sake! And then there's an outcry about jobs, England for the English, even though these guys would do work that the locals wouldn't touch anyway. But the main thing is, it's just the yobbos who've been moved in from the Tyne, they don't want these immigrants. And they do want trouble.'

'Some spilled over today?'

'Like a bloody dam bursting. The Black Horse, pub in Abbey. My guess is it was more or less all set up. The local roughnecks — little else to do with their giro cheques than drink in the pub — were waiting for these immigrant guys to show. When they did, they oiled into them. Did a pretty good wrecking job in the pub, but what they hadn't expected was that some of our lads would be there, trying to enjoy themselves.'

'And the lads did enjoy themselves, by wading in.' Culpeper grinned. 'Your youngsters, it would have made their day, really. Would have done for us, in the old times.'

Macardle chuckled in appreciative agreement. 'I suppose so. My lads quite enjoyed the dust-up, I think. And we're still interviewing the people concerned. That's why some of my senior officers aren't here.'

'You made some arrests and brought the villains here?' Culpeper asked in surprise.

Macardle grunted in vague disapproval. 'The local bobbies didn't really want to know. Someone got in touch with the Assistant Chief at Morpeth and he rang me. Asked if I could deal with it.'

'Why?'

Macardle winked. 'Come on, you know the ACC. He wouldn't want to have noisy files on his desk. Trouble of this kind — arising from government policy — he wouldn't want the publicity. He's looking forward to a gong one of these days and he wants his nose kept clean. So, he suggested if I handled it, kept it low-key . . . For once, I *have* to admit, it seemed a good idea, really. I mean, we don't want to trundle these characters across to Ponteland or Morpeth. Just a local fracas anyway. And I've got senior — albeit ageing — officers, who can handle the interviews. And good experience for some of the young cubs. Not the ones who took part in the hammering, of course. We got to retain objectivity, don't we?'

Culpeper laughed. 'Like always. So you're treating this as a training exercise!'

'Oh, we'll warn the buggers, let them cool their heels a while. Got some makeshift cells where they can wait. We're not having any of that solicitor stuff, of course, though one of your old friends has been shouting the odds.'

'Who's that?' Culpeper asked curiously.

'Sid Larson,' Macardle replied, eyeing Culpeper wickedly.

'That old bastard! You got him banged up downstairs?' Culpeper finished his drink. 'This I got to see.'

* * *

Three small seminar rooms had been commandeered for the interviews. A small window panel was set in the door of each, which made it convenient for Culpeper to be shown some of the individuals involved in the battle. Macardle gestured towards the three men huddled in the first room, disconsolate, bruised but projecting an air of weary defiance. 'They're the illegals,' Macardle explained. 'We'll be letting them out when it's safe to do so. We got most of the other louts off the premises already, with a warning. They'll be back inside, no doubt, quicker than a shake of a mare's tail, but not here.'

'These immigrants, where are they from?' Culpeper asked.

'Croatia, it seems. Unpronounceable names. The lads call them Ali, Tonto, and the Wolf Man.' When Culpeper raised his eyebrows, Macardle shrugged. 'You tell me. The Wolf Man, because he sank his teeth into one of the yobbos. That's the big one, with the angry face. He was the leader, seems like.'

Culpeper inspected him through the small window. Dark hair, dark features, broad shoulders under a leather jacket. After a few moments, the man raised his head and stared at Culpeper. His eyes were cold in their defiance. A hard man, Culpeper guessed. A man who'd seen trouble, and made trouble.

He nodded towards the prisoners. 'You'll release them soon.'

'Like I said, we've interviewed them, and they claim that they were just going in there for a drink. They got set upon. It had been coming for a while and they knew it. But the big character, the Wolf Man, he was up for it. Had enough, it seems. But my guess is we'll make a report, let them out, and it won't be long before they'll be heading back south. One way or another. Anyway, your old mucker's in here.'

He tapped on the door, led the way in, and the two officers in the room stood to attention, immediately. 'Not giving you too much trouble, is he?' Macardle asked affably.

'Just about finishing the statement, sir.'

Macardle beamed, and turned to the prisoner. 'Brought someone to see you, chew the fat over old times.'

The man in the torn polo-necked sweater stared at Culpeper. One of his eyes was almost closed, and his short-cropped, iron-grey hair was matted with dried blood at the crown. His lip was swollen. Culpeper shook his head in admonition. 'Now then, Sidney, old bugger like you, what you think you're up to?'

There was a short silence. A certain puzzlement crept into the man's sullen eyes; slowly, recognition dawned. He licked his swollen lip. 'Culpeper,' he croaked.

'The same.' Culpeper shook his head. 'I'm amazed. You still at it? I would've thought you learned your lesson years ago. But nothing's changed, hey?'

'We Brits got to stick up for our birth right,' Sid Larson snarled.

'Bullshit,' Culpeper disagreed pleasantly. 'You just like a good punch-up. Always did. Lemme see, I got to think way back. Hell, Sidney, I first came across you in the seventies! Those student riots you got involved in.'

Macardle raised his eyebrows in surprise, glancing between Culpeper and the surly prisoner. 'Never in the world. You were never a student, were you, Larson?'

Larson did not deign to answer the question, and Culpeper chuckled. 'No, of course not it's just the students fronted the riots . . . it was over some pit closures, I remember. You'll recall what it was like in those days . . . No, Sidney here, he wasn't a student but he didn't half work well. Winding them up from behind when they charged the police lines. Few heads got broken, didn't they, Sidney?'

'Police brutality,' Larson muttered. 'Treading on the faces of the masses.'

Culpeper sighed. 'But not yours. You always scarpered before we could lay hands on you. I could never work it out, Sidney. Were you an anarchist, a communist, or a fascist? I never got that one clear. Or was it that you just like putting in the boot?' He shook his head sadly. 'I just don't understand. You must be fifty now. And you're still behaving like a young tearaway. But you did it better in the old days. Then you were back behind, urging them on. Now, you take a hammering yourself, up front, it seems.'

'I always took it as well as gave it,' Larson said sourly. 'I stood up to be counted.'

'The hell you did! You were the first to run, once the fire was really alight. You were always the guy who picked the fight, threw the first chair, then got the hell out of there when it really got started.'

There was a short, disagreeable silence. Then Larson said in a grumbling tone, 'Them grunts are animals. One of them bit me — the big bastard. Took a chunk out of me leg.'

'I bet he spit it out again,' Culpeper suggested pleasantly.

'Unsavoury morsel,' Macardle agreed.

Culpeper grinned. 'Anyway, just called in to pay respects, for the sake of old times. See you around, no doubt, Sidney.'

'Not if I see you first,' Larson growled.

Culpeper nodded sagely. 'But that was always the way of it, wasn't that so? Like I said, you were always a better runner than a fighter. But now, what is it? Don't have the legs you used to?'

As he left the room with Macardle, Culpeper looked back and had the pleasure of seeing Larson mouth the word *bastard*.

Macardle closed the door, and stopped outside the third seminar room. Culpeper glanced in through the window. His eyes widened in surprise. He looked at Macardle, then opened the door, stuck his head into the room, to stare at the man being interviewed by the young officer.

'What the hell are *you* doing here? Don't tell me *you've* been involved in racist riots!'

* * *

'Do you have *any* idea at all, about the embarrassment you've caused the department?'

Karen Stannard was incandescent in her fury. Arnold was never certain about the colour of her eyes: it seemed to change with her mood. But right now, as she stood facing him in her room, they seemed to flash with the deep hard blue of ice. She was trembling in her rage, quivering with anger, and he thought that she had never seemed so beautiful. There was that quality about her. In calmer moments, when she was seeking to achieve her ends by subtle means, she could exude a feline sensuality. Her glance could be provocative and playful, she knew how to use the lines of her body to persuasive effect; and when anger came it could be cold, hard and unforgiving as she played the part of the ice queen. But this was a different kind of anger: fire and ice. It puzzled him somewhat.

'I mean, what the bloody hell do you think you were doing?' she stormed. 'I don't understand. How even you could manage to turn attendance at a funeral into a fist fight in a pub!'

Arnold shrugged uneasily. 'It was just . . . well, it just happened . . . Really, it was sort of unavoidable.'

'Unavoidable?' She glared at him in baffled dismay. 'Have you *seen* yourself?'

He had. His left eye was puffy where an elbow had struck him. There was an ugly, dark bruise along the side of his jaw. His mouth was swollen, and he was still aware of the salt taste of blood on his tongue. He spoke with difficulty and the appropriate words were not easy to find.

Karen Stannard had called him into her office as soon as he had arrived at work that morning.

'You're a senior officer in my department,' she raged. 'I'm away for just a week, and I come back to find you've got yourself involved in a fist fight in a Northumberland pub, the police have been involved, you've been interviewed—'

'There'll be no official action taken,' he intervened weakly, remembering the sight of Culpeper's surprised eyes when he had entered the seminar room, and the discussion they had had.

'That's not the point!' Karen Stannard hissed. 'You're the deputy head of this department and in my absence you behave like a common thug. You get involved in a racist disturbance. You get arrested, for God's sake! At least Chris Hayman had the sense to stay out of the way, not get involved! But you — you have to get stuck right in the middle of it all. You represent the department, don't you realize that? You were acting head at that point of time. You've let us down badly, are you aware of that? If I had my way I'd suspend you!'

Arnold was silent. It was best to let the sound and thunder swirl around him. But he was puzzled. It was appropriate that she should reprimand him. He knew that would be coming. But there was an edge to her fury he could not understand. It was personal, rather than professional.

Finally, when she had had her say, and his silence suggested contrition, she began to calm down. She sat behind her desk, glowering at him, her breasts heaving passionately under her white blouse. She brushed a stray wisp of hair away from her eyes and took a deep breath. 'You're on report, Arnold. The Chief Executive must be informed. I'm not carrying any cans for you. If the press get hold of this . . .' She eyed his bruises malevolently. 'God, what a picture you make . . . !'

Arnold remained silent, conscious of his swollen jaw and sore tongue. At last, reluctantly, she gestured towards the chair in front of her desk. 'Sit down.'

He obeyed. She faced him squarely for a little while, arms folded, staring at him in displeasure, her glance dwelling on each element of his facial injuries. She shook her head, sighing at the stupidity of men. 'I intended calling you in this morning, as soon as I got back from London, to give you good news. And then I walk into this story! However . . . Whether you're interested or not, the meetings I attended in London proved to be successful. We've been given the go-ahead to make a formal application for funding. It had been my intention to ask you to oversee the project. Now, I'm not sure whether you'll be able to tear yourself away sufficiently from your pugilistic enterprises to allow me to trust you with the work.'

Arnold opened his mouth to dispute the point, but thought better of it. She eyed him sourly.

'I'm designating the project Landslip, just like the television programme. It's a catchy name that the councillors liked. But I'm reluctant to let you handle it alone. So I'm staying in charge, personally — and that doesn't make me too happy, when I've got to run the department. This should have been something I could delegate to you, totally. But after this ridiculous behaviour . . .'

He waited.

'So, I'm splitting up the work. On reflection, I've decided that Portia Tyrrel can take on responsibility for the work at Roundsay, and at the Devil's Hole. I don't want you wandering all over the place from one site to another, and stopping off at pubs in between for the odd punch-up with the locals.'

Her eyes seemed to glow darkly as she watched him, waiting for reaction. He gave her his studied indifference look.

She sniffed imperiously. 'So you'll concentrate on the sea cave. There's the defences to build, and you'll liaise with the Public Works people on that. And there's a big cataloguing job to do in the cave itself, now it's been opened up. Anyway, the fact is, I've made notes on the project. I want you to write up the details, make the necessary investigations on site, consult various authorities who might be able to assist . . . such as Professor Davidson at the University of Newcastle, and so on. But I want to be kept informed, every step of the way. *Every step*. I don't want to find that you've left things undone because you've started some other world title fight in some grotty pub back of beyond.'

He wanted to tell her she was being unfair. He decided it wasn't worth it.

'So, the details are in the file. You've no doubt heard of much of it, but get up to speed with it, start preparing the project submission so we can make formal application for the grants, and, please, try to stay out of trouble.'

Which was more or less what Detective Chief Inspector Culpeper had suggested when he had spoken to Arnold in the police training centre. But at least Culpeper had seemed amused, rather than infuriated.

Duly chastened, Arnold returned to his office with the thick file on the Landslip Project under his arm. A couple of secretaries passed him in the corridor, and giggled. He sighed despondently: the department would be rife with rumours. He doubted his part in the fracas would be described as heroic. He placed the file on his desk, went out to get a cup of coffee from the machine at the end of the corridor, returned to his room and closed the door firmly behind him.

He sat down, opened the file, sipped his coffee, and shut out all thoughts of his recent troubles as he familiarized himself with the details of the Landslip Project.

The sea cave at Abbey Head had been discovered only a year ago. The last winter had been particularly violent in its weather. There had been severe storms along the northeast coast, defences had been breached in numerous places, and heavy rain had caused a considerable amount of erosion on the cliff faces all along the coastline. One of the areas to suffer badly was the headland itself. There had been a landslip as a result of the undercutting force of the sea and an entrance had been torn out of the rock by the spring tides. Some amateurs from a local rambling group, walking along the shoreline, had decided to investigate and had made a surprising discovery: they had identified carvings and paintings in the cave. They had no idea how old they were.

The notes Karen Stannard had supplied in the file made the problems clear. There was no record of the existence of the sea cave prior to the discovery. There was no entry from the sea to the cave prior to the discovery, and yet it was said by the potholers that the cave contained evidence of human use. She had scribbled in the margin at one point that there was the possibility that there had been an entrance in antiquity, but that it had been hidden by an ancient rock fall, which had now been eroded by the storms of recent years.

What was required was a close investigation of the cave, an identification — and preservation — of the carvings and paintings, and resolution of the problem that faced any such investigation: the likelihood of the cave being damaged, sealed again or flooded by the activity of the crashing waves of the northern sea.

She had outlined, during her discussions in London, some of the defensive work that was necessary: she had also suggested what it would cost. The tick placed beside the sum in her notes seemed to suggest that there was a strong likelihood that the money would be made available from central sources. There was a rough sketch of the site, together with a proposal for the construction of a sea wall to protect the site from encroaching waves. Arnold had to admit she seemed to have done her homework well, and the mandarins and politicians in London would have been impressed.

And now it was over to him. As for her supervising his work, he had doubts about the reality of that. He could guess what it would really mean: Karen Stannard had never been slow, coming forward to claim credit. But if there were to be a problem . . . she would have Arnold as a scapegoat. There was nothing new in that situation. He sighed. He'd been there before.

He looked at the action notes on the last sheet of the file papers.

Contact Daniel Gibbs.
Determine Hall Gabriel situation.
Sea Caves of Antiquity . . . third edition 1999 Prof
Davidson.

There was a light tap on the door. Arnold rose, stretched, pushed the file aside and went to the door, opened it. Chris Hayman was standing there, stocky, vaguely belligerent, a somewhat sheepish look on his face. 'Can I have a word?'

Arnold was still stung by the fact that once the fighting had started, Hayman had disappeared: he had managed to keep his nose clean with the head of the department. Arnold was inclined to tell him to get lost, but he remembered the man's recent bereavement, and shrugged and turned aside. Hayman followed him into the room and stood in front of Arnold's desk. 'I . . . I hear you've been in to see Miss Stannard.'

'News travels fast in the department.'

'I gather she was more than a little mad.'

'More than a little.'

There was a short silence. Hayman seemed ill at ease, trying to find the right words. He inspected Arnold's bruises. 'You took a bit of a pasting.'

'I did.'

'I'm sorry.'

Arnold leaned back in his chair, somewhat exasperated. He inspected Hayman's own features: they were unmarked. 'You seem to have got out of it well enough.' Hayman shuffled anxiously. 'When you dragged me back, I got thrown to one side. Everything was . . . confused. I knew you were in the middle of it, and when those young coppers piled in, well, I was sort of on the fringe, and it didn't seem . . . wise, to get involved. Then I saw one of them calling for support, so . . .'

'Discretion suggested you fade away,' Arnold suggested coldly.

'There really wasn't much I could have done to help,' Hayman said guardedly.

'Not at that stage, maybe. But it would have been better if you hadn't started it!'

Hayman straightened, angrily. 'I didn't start it! It was obviously all planned. That group of men at the table, they were waiting for those immigrants to come into the pub. There was always going to be a battle. It was they who started it—'

'That's not quite the way I saw it,' Arnold disagreed grimly. 'What the hell got into you, hitting the man like that?'

'I don't recall hitting him,' Hayman replied sullenly. 'You said something to him, and then all hell seemed to break loose.'

There was a short silence. The colour seemed to have drained from Hayman's features and his eyes were vague. He shrugged, diffidently. 'I was . . . upset. Not thinking straight. The funeral . . . And then, I don't know what got into me. I suppose I did say something, but . . .'

'What did you say?' Arnold asked curiously. Hayman's glance fluttered around the room, as though searching for a way to escape. 'I suppose . . . I think I might have said something . . . insulting. About his country. Or that he was an illegal. It was . . . just a reaction. I was upset.'

'I didn't understand what you said,' Arnold muttered accusingly. 'But it made the man in the leather jacket react.'

'He made a comment about my family,' Hayman said bleakly.

'In what language?'

Hayman grimaced. 'I spoke to him in Polish.' He hesitated. 'It was my mother . . . she taught me a little. Most of it has gone now. It was all a long time ago. Anyway . . .' He licked his lips nervously, looking at the floor. 'I came in to . . . apologize.'

Arnold was suddenly irritated by the whole thing. He waved his hand. 'Forget it. It's not important.'

'It wouldn't have happened but for . . .'

Arnold understood. The funeral. The loss of his wife. Pent-up grief, and tension. More gently, he said, 'I told you, Chris. Forget it. It's all over.'

He still stood there. He raised his eyes slowly. 'Are you going to be disciplined?'

Arnold grunted in dissatisfaction. 'Let's say I've been hauled over the coals. But it's not anything I can't handle.'

'Did . . . did my name come up?'

Arnold took a deep breath. This would be the real reason why Hayman came to see him. Not to apologize, but to discover what had been said in Karen Stannard's office, find out whether any blame had been put on Hayman, and whether he also was likely to face Karen Stannard. She could certainly unnerve a man, Arnold thought grimly to himself. He shook his head. 'Somehow,' he said quietly, 'your name just didn't come up.'

Chris Hayman straightened a little, bobbed his head slowly. 'Thanks. I . . . I owe you one.'

'I told you. Forget it.'

After all, Arnold considered after Hayman had left the office, such a situation was hardly likely to arise again. Next time, Karen Stannard could attend the funeral herself.

He worked a little more on the file, and then decided he would go to the departmental library archives to see if there was a copy of Professor Davidson's *Sea Caves of Antiquity* among the holdings. The librarian soon found it for him, and he checked it out to his name. He was walking back to his office when someone called his name. He turned. It was Portia Tyrrel.

It was said among staff in the other departments that there was one considerable perquisite to working in the Department of Museums and Antiquities. The work might involve poring over dusty remains, old maps and texts, and scrabbling around in dark corners of archaeological digs — but who wouldn't be prepared to do that in the company of the two most beautiful women in the county?

And Portia Tyrrel was beautiful — although not like Karen Stannard was beautiful. The two women were quite different: the head of department tall, cool, confident, almost arrogant in her classical beauty, turning the head of every man when she entered a room. But Portia Tyrrel turned heads too. She was smaller than Karen, slighter, slimmer. She barely topped five feet two; her black, shiny hair was cut short, fringed, setting off the pale olive of her skin — the legacy of her Singaporean mother. Her smile was perfect; even, white teeth. She was sharp, intelligent and ambitious: officially Karen Stannard's assistant, she had subtly carved out areas of activity for herself which widened the scope of her power within the department. Both women were beautiful; both were ruthless; both were controlled and calculating. Arnold had had reason, as far as Portia was concerned, to experience that calculation, one sunny afternoon, in the long, sweet grass of the fell.

Inevitably, when he was surprised by Portia, his thoughts swept back briefly to that afternoon, and his pulse rate changed.

'So, Arnold, you've been in the wars.'

She reached forward and touched his mouth lightly; her fingers were slim and cool.

'Rough and tumble. Nothing serious.'

'Not what I heard.' She smiled at him appraisingly. 'I like a man who can stand up for himself.'

'It wasn't exactly my fight.'

'Karen thinks you shouldn't even have been there.'

'So do I.'

'But you didn't shop Chris Hayman.' Her glance was provocative. 'Rumours get around . . . and it's said he got out of the way while you took the bruising. And how was Karen about it all.'

'Berserk,' Arnold replied, smiling in spite of himself.

Portia linked her arm in his in a possessive gesture as they walked along the corridor together. He was aware of the subtle hint of her perfume. 'Yes, I've had a meeting with her — she's been explaining to me about Roundsay and the Devil's Hole. It's something I'll enjoy doing. Of course, I would rather have worked with you again, Arnold. I did suggest it, in fact. But she was still much too angry to listen. Have you thought much about her anger?'

He shrugged. 'A bit over the top, I suppose.'

'And you didn't realize why?' she giggled, gripping his arm conspiratorially.

'What do you mean?'

'Well, you don't really think it was just about the reputation of the department, do you, Arnold? Or the fact that she might be embarrassed about publicity? Oh, come on!'

Arnold stopped, turned to face her. Her dark eyes were mischievous. 'I don't understand.'

'It was *concern*,' she whispered, leaning towards him so that her face was close to his. 'She was concerned about you. Didn't you realize that?'

She laughed, a low, melodious, chuckling sound, and then she turned, headed for the stairs. As her heels echoed down the stairwell Arnold heard a sound at the end of the corridor. He turned, looked towards Karen Stannard's room. His head of department was standing there in the open doorway, expressionlessly. She stared at him for several seconds, her glance stony, and then she closed the door.

Arnold groaned mentally. He had no doubt in his mind that Portia's taking his arm had been a deliberate act. The whispering in his ear, the giggling, they were all part of the same process. His guess was it was always her intention that Karen Stannard should have seen their conspiratorial looking discussion. It was all part of a deliberate game Portia Tyrrel played, driven by the same kind of motives that had led her to seduce Arnold on the high fell that sunny afternoon.

It was not about him; it was about power.

3

Taking over the new project did not mean that Arnold was freed from his other commitments: as the acknowledged deputy to Karen Stannard he was forced to get involved in a great deal more committee work than he had previously undertaken — she delegated to him the less important committees — and there was the usual range of supervisory work on other projects to be continued. He realized that the Landslip Project had to be given a certain priority, so he first of all contacted the Public Works Department to arrange a meeting regarding construction work. They directed him towards the Planning Department because of certain access problems they envisaged. The final frustration was attempting to contact Professor Saul Davidson. The professor's secretary at the university informed Arnold in a cool, superior voice that the professor was in Israel at the moment, and would not be returning for another week. She somewhat reluctantly entered an appointment for him, to be confirmed later, in the professor's diary.

At least Arnold was thereafter able to get out of the office for a few days, doing what he most enjoyed. There were two digs he had to visit: one was located near Hareshaw Dene, where the burn flowed through a wooded valley to Hareshaw

Linn, the waterfall tumbling into a rocky amphitheatre at the head of the gorge. A small team was working there, looking for traces of Stone Age man: Arnold was acting in liaison with the National Park Authority and kept notes of the project for his departmental archives. The other dig took him further north, near Carter Bar, the highest point on any road between England and Scotland, where wide-ranging views northward embraced much of the Scottish lowlands, while to the west and south dark plantations spread into the distance.

These were the drives he liked best: the opportunity to get away from his desk, cross deep valleys cut into limestone and millstone grit, note the colour contrast between the high horizon moors and fells and the lush green of the grassy dales. He found a small hotel tucked away near the site of the dig, where they were investigating the earthworks built by the Celtic Brigantes, the old people of the Pennine moors and dales, where they might well have taken their last stand against the invading Roman soldiers. He was able to spend the afternoon at the dig, discussing the range of finds, and in the evening there was the comfort of the sixteenth-century inn, a good dinner and a bottle of wine, and Professor Davidson's *Sea Caves of Antiquity* to read.

The work was not a dry, academic tome. Davidson used an almost lyrical tone in discussing his chosen topic, and ranged widely from chthonic cults in Mongolia to artificial caves and grottoes in China. He dealt with locations in Greece and abysmal chasms in Crete. He covered Minoan and Buddhist cultures, and touched upon the subterranean passages of Teotihuacan. He considered how sensory deprivation was the key to producing altered states of consciousness for the shaman in his deep, inky-dark grotto. Davidson saw the sea caves not only as habitations and shelters for early man, but also the first cathedrals, the entrance to the underworld, the liminal place where earth light ended and the eternal darkness began. He saw the cave as a metaphor: at the same time the womb of the earth, and also the gateway to the realm of the dead. Davidson wrote well: as he read the powerfully worded prose, Arnold imagined he could almost feel the chill silence of a cavernous night, living at the boundary between the living world of men and the mysterious, dark realms of the shades and the sorcerer and the shaman. Davidson ranged in his study from discussion of palaeolithic paintings — *frozen visions on the walls of prehistory* — to the initiation rites that would have been practised in the caves, where men wrestled with the spirits between light and dark, life and death, sight and vision.

When he finished the book late that night in his bedroom, Arnold felt he was looking forward to meeting the man who had written it. His assistance would indeed be valuable in the investigation of the sea cave at Abbey Head.

The meeting with his colleagues from Planning and Public Works the following week was somewhat frustrating. They lacked his enthusiasm for the project. They seemed more inclined to raise problems than produce solutions. They talked endlessly of work schedules, equipment availability, time scales and manpower shortages. Consequently, when Karen Stannard called for his first report, he had little to offer her.

'What the hell's been going on?' she demanded coldly.

'Bureaucracy,' Arnold explained. 'You know — the ability to make no decisions and accept no responsibility.'

'We'll see about that,' Karen Stannard hissed. 'There's money involved here.'

She was on the phone immediately to the Chief Executive. An appointment was fixed for that afternoon. She took Arnold in with her and told the Chief Executive that Arnold would explain.

He did. Powell Frinton was nearing the end of his long stint as Chief Executive now: lean, thin-skinned, easily bored and often frustrated by the need to sort out departmental squabbles, he was well aware of the tensions that had existed between Arnold and Karen Stannard and it was obvious to Arnold that he wondered whether this matter arose from that source. But he promised to issue instructions to the relevant teams, for he clearly understood the importance of the funding — he had, after all, been one of the group that had negotiated the sum in London.

'However,' he said, pursing his thin lips in doubt, 'I have received a communication from the Public Works people that raises a slightly awkward issue. You say that it will be necessary to build a sea wall, in order to protect the cave entrance.'

Arnold nodded. 'High tides were responsible for opening up the cave — that, and cliff erosion over the years. But I understand now the danger is that unless we have a retaining wall the cave itself could be scoured clean in winter storms.'

Powell Frinton pinched the end of his narrow nose thoughtfully. 'The problem is that I have a note here from the Public Works people to the effect that it is not possible to get the necessary heavy machinery down to the beach area. Not directly, that is. There is no road down, except some three miles to the north, at Roundsay Cove, and then there are the sands, the rocks, which are claimed to be treacherous and difficult—'

'To Public Works, all things are difficult,' Karen Stannard muttered.

Powell Frinton raised an elegant eyebrow, but then decided to refrain from rising to that particular bait.

'I've been looking at the Ordnance Survey map for the area,' Arnold suggested, 'and it seems to me there is an old track running across the headland and down to the beach.'

Powell Frinton nodded. 'It's a very old track. This is mentioned by Public Works. But the track is not a public right of way. It crosses private land. Abbey Manor. That means you would have to enter into negotiations with the owners.'

'I've already looked into the matter,' Karen Stannard announced. 'The owner is called Gibbs. And the land is up for sale. I was wondering . . . in view of the importance of the site, access to the sea cave, the ruined abbey itself as well as the manor house . . .'

'Yes?' Powell Frinton asked coldly.

'Maybe we should be taking the matter to the council. If the authority were to purchase the land—'

'You are now head of the department,' Powell Frinton intoned with a measured severity. 'You must by now be aware that expenditure of that kind is completely out of the question in the present state of our finances. The amounts allocated to the Department of Museums and Antiquities are already far overstretched.'

'It would be an asset,' Karen replied stubbornly.

'It would be a liability,' Powell Frinton disagreed.

'So we'd better talk to Mr Gibbs about access,' Arnold suggested in the frosty silence that followed.

* * *

The view from the top of the old pele tower of Abbey Manor was impressive. Below them the wide sweep of the headland, grazed by sheep, sloped gently in a green swathe eastwards towards the rocky cliff that plunged down to the sea. A short distance from the edge of the cliff stood the stark, romantic outline of the abbey ruins, blackly gazing out to the distant horizon. The afternoon sun had created a haze which restricted the outlook seawards, beyond the ruined abbey, but Arnold could make out the dark mass of an offshore container ship, and some smaller boats of the fishing fleet from Amble, black shapes against the intense blue of the sea. Westwards lay a stonewalled pattern of fields; enclosures that would date back to the medieval period, farmed still by smallholdings, sheep, cattle and pigs. Further west, against a purpling, darkening sky where a storm threatened, was the hulk of the Cheviot and to the north were the vague outlines of the Scottish lowlands.

'It's beautiful,' Karen Stannard breathed. 'It must be a wrench to part with all this.'

'Economics,' Daniel Gibbs replied in a matter-of-fact tone. 'Yes, it is a wrench, of course, after all the land has been in the family for generations. But, one has to face the facts of life. My father sold off some of the farms out there to pay death duties. His father had done the same before him. So the actual landholding now is much reduced. And as for Abbey Manor itself, well you can guess that it costs a hell of a lot to keep up. This tower, for instance, badly needs repair — crumbling stone, damaged foundations. I wouldn't normally bring people up here, but since this is your first visit, you have to see the view . . .'

'How old is the abbey?' Arnold asked.

'Eleventh-century I believe. I don't know that it had that long a history really. The original foundation was established with financial assistance from one of the old Templars, de Burgh — who was trying to make certain of the absolution that he felt desirable after all the casque-bashing activity he'd indulged in over the years. The monks promised to pray for him for three hundred years. I don't know whether it was a good bargain, but de Burgh seemed to think so, even if his sons didn't. They had to go back to institutional mayhem to make a living for themselves.'

'Way of life.' Karen murmured.

Gibbs nodded. 'The land gave the abbey support — sheep and wool were major commodities — and there was a market, I believe, in Abbey village itself, but that's long since come to an end. There was a proposal at one time, before my father died, to start it up again as a sort of summer fair, but nothing came of it. No, the abbey came crashing down well before Henry VIII started his own demolition job, and ever since it's been somewhat of a struggle. Our family bought the estate out of Georgian brewery money, but that's also long past. Families rise and fall, don't they? My ancestors might have been wealthy from brewing ale, but I'm afraid the Gibbs family has been on a gentle downward slope for a long while now. Personally, I think it all started when Abbey Manor was purchased. But there you are, ideas of grandeur, the nouveaux riches . . .'

Arnold considered the abbey ruins with interest: from what he could make out at this distance, the ancient abbey had been built in the standard monastic church pattern of the time: a large-aisled nave, a western arch with two smaller arches either side of the nave altar. All ruined now, its roof gone, a hint of the vaulted refectory, gap-toothed walls. 'A Romanesque rectangle as opposed to a Byzantine square construction,' Arnold murmured. 'Pseudo-cruciform. A good example of work completed during the Ottonian renaissance period—'

'Arnold,' Karen warned, eyeing him balefully. She turned to smile sweetly at their host. 'It really is good of you to give us this little tour.'

Daniel Gibbs had been quite helpful when Arnold telephoned him and explained the situation. He had been vaguely non-committal with regard to the use of the track to the beach, but had suggested the best plan would be for Arnold to come out to Abbey Manor and discuss with him exactly what was being proposed. He had heard of the discovery of the sea cave, of course, and was by inclination supportive of archaeological work, but the matter might shortly be taken out of his hands, since there was a prospective buyer for the land and matters were near completion. But even so, it might be as well to have discussions, and he had invited Arnold to call. When Arnold had made his report to Karen Stannard, she had decided to come along.

They had used Arnold's car and driven north-west from Morpeth. Necessarily, they had to drive through Abbey village — Arnold had kept his eyes straight ahead when they passed the Black Horse — but his passenger had made no comment, though he was aware that she stared balefully at his fading bruises at the time. They drove on between high, neatly trimmed hedges towards the rise of the headland where Abbey Manor stood. They caught a glimpse of it as they came past the ruined abbey itself, stark on the headland: the house was probably sixteenth-century, Arnold guessed. Square in construction, it sat solidly at the end of a gravelled drive, a monument to the pride of a family confident in their landholding and place in society. To one side of the ivy-clad main hall a pele tower had been constructed, providing a wide view of the countryside and protection for the owners in times of emergency. There would have been many of those, in the turbulent years of the Debatable Land.

Daniel Gibbs had met them on the steps of the manor house. He was of middle height, about forty years of age, tanned, a hint of grey at his temples, silvering his dark hair. He had craggy features and a slightly reserved air. He had become slightly less reserved after he was introduced to Karen Stannard. His shoulders seemed to straighten somewhat, and his head came up so that he could show he was slightly taller than her. Early in the conversation he found cause to mention that he had been married but no longer was so, and shortly afterwards the invitation to look around the premises was suddenly extended to joining him for dinner at the manor house.

Gibbs took them on a tour of the manor house. He largely ignored Arnold as he led Karen around, showing her the magnificent oak staircase, the vaulted roof of the chapel, the sixteenth-century library, and the ivy-trailed pele tower that had served as a barricade for the owners against the marauding raids of the Scots.

'My father was very interested in the history of the pele tower, of course,' Gibbs explained. 'Because of his background, I suppose. He was a major in the army. A bit disappointed in the end, I think, because my grandfather was a brigadier at the close of his army career, but my father never rose higher than major. And his career ended somewhat prematurely . . . but in retirement he wrote a small book on the border raids, you know, and did quite a lot of investigation of the peles in the area. Never was much interested myself. I trained as an accountant,' he added, almost apologetically. 'And maybe that was why I've held a less than, romantic view of the place. Running it now, it just doesn't make sense financially.'

'You say you've found a purchaser?' Arnold asked.

'Well, yes, I have. All done and dusted it seems, bar the final contractual details. A man called Hall Gabriel. Businessman. Reckons he used to live around here. Started his business not ten miles from here. Moved away in his thirties, prospered, and now wants to come back. Though whether he'll just use the place as a holiday home or not, I don't know. I mean, you can't really do business from here, I wouldn't think.' He had scratched at his prow of a nose, reflectively. 'If you ask me, I think Mr Gabriel is on a sort of nostalgia trip. Anyway, you'll get to meet him.'

'Today?' Karen asked in surprise.

Gibbs smiled at her. 'He's due here this evening, for dinner. So we could talk over final details. Now you're staying, you'll have the chance to meet him. Kill two birds with one stone, then, hey? And I can't imagine he'll be offended by your presence.'

Arnold was beginning to think it had been a good idea that Karen had decided to come to Abbey Manor with him.

They finished their tour of the house and Gibbs offered them a drink in the library. They served themselves — the servants were part time, Gibbs apologized — and they admired the view from the tall library windows. The shadows were lengthening across the headland when Gibbs glanced at his watch. 'Mr Gabriel will be here in an hour or so, and dinner won't be until seven. I wonder whether you'd be interested in a little stroll? There's something else I'd like to show you.'

They agreed, and finished their drinks. Daniel Gibbs led them out of the manor house and across the field beyond, towards the headland and the abbey. He walked ahead with Karen, talking animatedly, clearly out to impress. Arnold followed behind more slowly, admiring the outline of the scarred abbey ruins against the sky. With this outlook, the abbey would probably have been erected because the headland would always have had some sacred significance: it had been the way of Christianity from the beginning. Churches, abbeys, cathedrals, they had often been erected at pagan sites,

47

locations that already had importance for local people. It was a way of claiming an inheritance, and of demonstrating superiority, but it also had the practical intention of taking advantage of prehistory.

Arnold became aware they were nearing the edge of the cliff, as the sound of booming surf became clearer. 'It's just along here,' he heard Gibbs say.

A few moments later Gibbs held up a hand in warning. 'I suppose it should really be fenced off, but we've not had any sheep falling in. Not in my time, anyway. Here it is, the other pride of Abbey Manor. The Well of Time, some have called it. Others call it Hades Gate.'

Arnold stepped forward. The chasm was fringed with fern and long, lank grass, the rock formation at its mouth curious in its bubbling effect. Two ledges ran along its curved sides, lifting as though carved, labia on a primitive organ, and the black depths gaped coldly to the afternoon sunlight.

'Old maps have a ruder name for it, of course,' Daniel Gibbs said, with a quick glance at Karen Stannard. 'And there's a kind of local legend which has it that the chasm represents the earth mother. But it's all a bit confused, between birth and death, you know what I mean?'

'How deep is it?' Karen asked, leaning forward at the edge to peer downwards.

'Who knows?' Gibbs replied. 'But deep. As a kid I used to toss stones down, and the echoes went on for ever.'

'No one investigated it?' Arnold queried. 'No potholers?'

Gibbs shrugged. 'My father fielded a few requests but turned them down, even though they said they were covered by their own insurance. Private land, he said, and that was it. But locals have walked these cliffs often enough, and it's well enough known. But it's a place that's always given me the shudders. I've heard the noises, you see.'

'Noises?' Karen Stannard turned to face him. 'What sort of noises?'

Daniel Gibbs was enjoying himself. 'When I was a kid, I came up here one evening and it was like a howling, wolf-like.

It was a pretty wild night, and maybe it was my imagination, but it scared the hell out of me at the time. I told my father, and he explained that he'd heard it too, and that the pit was all tied up with local stories about the talking mouth, the booming of devils, the crying of women. He said he'd read that priests had been up here to exorcize the cave spirits in the old days, that it was sometimes consulted almost like an oracle, that there were old women who prayed here in times gone by. There's a seventeenth-century text — they have it at Newcastle University — which reckons that witches were cast into the pit here, to enter the gateway of their master.'

'Hades Gate,' Arnold said.

'That's right. As for the Well of Time . . .' Gibbs shrugged. 'Maybe that's just a reference to its antiquity.'

'How far away is the track down to the beach?' Arnold asked.

Gibbs turned, and gestured. 'Well, as you can see, there's a worn track running just along the edge of the headland. That's the only public right of way on the land. It leads to that lookout point over there — courting couples often park there on summer evenings. But the track doesn't go down to the beach.'

Gibbs waved his hand in a general sweep. 'This is all private, with no right of access apart from that track. But you see where the land rises just over there? The old track-way, and I think it's really old, you know, sort of used by the monks in ancient times, it runs along the ridge just there, and drops down through that ravine, down to the beach. It's the obvious way to get down to your sea cave, but if you want to take heavy machinery down there, the track will need some strengthening, particularly where it gets near the edge of the drop down to the rocks.'

'You think it's feasible?' Karen Stannard asked.

Gibbs gave her a smitten smile. 'Everything's possible, Karen. And if I were not selling the manor, I would certainly give permission. But, in the circumstances . . . Talking of which . . .' He consulted his watch. 'I think we'd better be going back. You'll probably want to have a wash and brush up. Then it will be time to meet the man who's likely to be the new owner of Abbey Manor and all it entails.'

* * *

They met in the library before dinner. From the room made available to him Arnold had seen the arrival of the Rolls. Two men had got out, to be greeted by Daniel Gibbs. They were introduced to Arnold and Karen over another round of drinks, as Hall Gabriel and Sean Corman.

'Mr Landon and Miss Stannard are employed by the local authority,' Gibbs explained. 'They wanted to discuss with me the possibility of using an old trackway on the headland to get access to the beach, to work on a retention wall, and investigate the cave itself.'

'Ah, yes, I'd read about that cave. But it wasn't known years ago.' His voice was deep, resonant, controlled and confident. Hall Gabriel was white-haired and in his mid-fifties but his handclasp and general build suggested to Arnold that the man was very fit. Possibly weekly bouts of squash would account for his muscular, well-honed appearance. He was dressed expensively, his suit well-cut, his shirt crisp, and he moved around the room with an already proprietorial air. But Arnold suspected Gabriel would always give that kind of impression. He was used to ownership, and expected to get his way.

The relationship between him and his companion was clear: Sean Corman, younger, alert and watchful, with eyes that never seemed to be still, was introduced as Gabriel's business associate, but there was no doubt that it was Gabriel who gave orders, and Corman who jumped to obey. Moreover, as Arnold noted the broken nose, the hard mouth and the light tread of the younger man he began to suspect that Corman's real usefulness would lie not so much in business acumen, as in physical support of some kind. Arnold's guess was that Corman would be used to troubleshooting, or concerned to make sure that no trouble came Hall Gabriel's way.

Over dinner Gabriel listened politely as Karen Stannard explained the purpose of their visit. Daniel Gibbs was entranced. He had made sure she was seated on his right so he could enjoy her proximity. Arnold watched from the other end of the table, where he was seated near Corman. Karen could use occasions like this with magnificent ease. Her body language was superb, her manipulation of her audience admirable. Arnold had seen it all before — with councillors, businessmen, colleagues. He was now touched with a certain cynicism about her performance, but he had to admit it was effective.

'And you, Daniel, you'd go along with these proposals?' Gabriel asked.

Gibbs almost fell over himself in his attempt to make Karen Stannard happy. 'I think I would have been only too happy to oblige. It'll be up to you, of course, Mr Gabriel, as the new owner of Abbey Manor, to make the decision, but opening up the trackway shouldn't cause you any great discomfort.'

'We'd make the inconvenience as little as possible,' Karen smiled at him. 'And we'd make good the area afterwards, of course.'

'Well, I'd be interested in seeing more detailed plans, of course, Miss Stannard, but I think I can say that — in principle at least — we can probably be supportive.' Karen Stannard glowed and shot a satisfied, triumphant glance in Arnold's direction.

Arnold sipped his wine. It was a good quality claret, he surmised. Daniel Gibbs would not be skimping this evening, in his eagerness to close the sale of Abbey Manor. 'You said earlier, Mr Gabriel, that you were not aware of the sea cave previously. The tone of your voice suggested you knew the area years ago.'

Gabriel turned his head to look at Arnold. He smiled slightly. 'I was brought up not too far from here. But in conditions far removed from Abbey Manor. I remember Major Gibbs — Daniel's father — owning the land. I used to do a bit of poaching in the woods just three miles from here. It was a time where, if Karen will excuse the expression, I had no arse in my trousers. Things changed after that. I started in business, I prospered, I moved away.'

'And now you're coming back.'

At the periphery of Arnold's vision Sean Corman moved. It was slight enough, a slow shifting in his seat, but Arnold was aware that Corman was staring at him. He glanced at Corman. The man's eyes were cold and intent, weighing up Arnold and perhaps finding him light in the balance, but watching him nevertheless.

Hall Gabriel was at ease. 'Well, yes, I'm intending to come back. Been intending for years. And when I heard Abbey Manor was up for sale . . . You must know how it is, Mr Landon? It's a common enough story. A man grows up in an area where he's known . . . not poverty exactly, but certainly the kind of life where money is scarce. And around him he sees others, landed gentlemen, like the major, for instance . . .'

Gibbs laughed, a little nervous tension in his voice. 'The old man was never exactly a landed gentleman. Not enough cash in hand for that kind of life.'

Gabriel ignored him, his glance fixed on Arnold, but looking at his own past. 'So a man can move away, build another life, become wealthy beyond his old dreams, but then, there comes a point in time when the past calls him. He remembers times, and places, and they belong to his youth. He wants to recall them. If he's lucky enough, he can.'

'And wealthy enough,' Arnold suggested.

'And wealthy enough,' Gabriel agreed slowly, holding Arnold's glance. 'Do you . . . disapprove of that kind of ambition, Mr Landon?'

Arnold became aware of Sean Corman moving again, leaning forward slightly, like a cat ready to pounce. 'Not at all,' he replied. 'I think it's an admirable attitude and one I can understand. To seek out the playgrounds of your youth. The trouble is, the things you remember are sometimes not quite what you thought they were. The past has a way of disappointing you.'

Gabriel smiled lazily, leaning back in his chair as he took a sip of the red wine. 'Oh, I don't think I'll be disappointed.'

'What exactly was your business?' Arnold asked. 'Transport, to start with. Then a bit of property development. In the old days.'

'That'll be what . . . the sixties, seventies? The time when all those building scandals were resounding through the north?'

There was a short silence. Karen Stannard was glaring at him, and perhaps justifiably. Arnold could not think why he had made the comment — perhaps it was the wine, perhaps it was the cool, confident arrogance of the man seated next to Daniel Gibbs. Or perhaps it was the presence of Carman, tensed for some indefinable reason across the table from him.

Gabriel's glance was calculating, as he hesitated, seeking the right words. Then he nodded, almost casually. 'Yes, there was a deal of corruption in those days. Local government officers sticking their fingers in the pie . . .' The slightly amused contempt in his eyes nettled Arnold. 'But you should realize, Mr Landon, there was no way I could be touched by that. I was too small in those days. I managed to get a bit of backing from an old friend and we went into the transport business, with a bit of house renovation thrown in. But we were small fry. We never got even a sniff of those rich local authority deals that were flying around in the redevelopment of Newcastle. So I came out clean from all that. Then, I had a bit of luck, bought out my partner — not long before he died, actually — and then moved away as the business expanded. London, Brussels, even Florida at one stage . . . it's remarkable how things expanded. But, in the end, the thought came . . . I'd like to come back to my roots.'

'Not permanently, of course,' Daniel Gibbs suggested nervously. 'I mean, around here you'd probably die of boredom if you lived here for any length of time.'

Gabriel chuckled. 'I've no desire to die for a long while yet, of any ailment. But, you're right — my business interests will keep me away for most of the time. But I'll have Abbey Manor to come back to. Whenever the feeling that I want to touch base with my youth again returns to me.'

'You're a lucky man, Mr Gabriel,' Arnold said carefully.

'I always have been, Mr Landon.'

Arnold had no doubt just what Karen Stannard would say when they made the drive back to Morpeth later that evening. And he was right.

'What on earth were you trying to say over dinner? Do you have to be so offensive and boorish?'

Yet Arnold could only think about the oily easiness of Hall Gabriel's smile, and the restrained tension in Sean Corman's body: a dog straining at a leash.

CHAPTER TWO

1

Professor Saul Davidson was perhaps six feet in height, spare of build, and slightly stooped. He was in his early fifties, Arnold guessed, but had retained a good head of hair which was dark, and barely streaked with grey. His features were lean, almost saturnine in appearance, quizzical eyebrows above humorous, pouched brown eyes that were neverthe-less careful in their appraisal. His skin was tanned and lined: deep cicatrices marked the edges of his mouth. Arnold gained the impression of a man who would always be careful about what he said, or divulged, but who could be a good friend in a crisis. His handshake was warm, his general demeanour welcoming.

'I'm sorry it's been so difficult to arrange a meeting, Mr Landon. I was at a conference in Israel last week, and when I got back, inevitably the paperwork had built up. And I had a report to prepare.' He smiled easily and gestured Arnold to a seat in the small, cramped, book-lined room at the univer-sity. He shook his head at the piles of paper that littered his desk. 'I have a secretary, but I'm afraid I have the bad habit of insisting that only I shift paper on my desk. Unfortunately, I'm not a tidy man — so, though it makes life easier for her, it actually makes life more difficult for me.' He reached into the drawer of his desk and extracted a pack of cigarettes. 'Do you mind?'

'Not at all.' It was Davidson's room, after all. 'I don't,' he added, as Davidson offered the extended pack to him.

'I need the calming effect it has on my nerves,' Davidson laughed. 'Dealing with students can sometimes be trying.'

'And you've been tried for quite a while here, I gather.'

Davidson cocked his head to one side, considering. 'I suppose it must be thirty-five years or so, now. I came here in the late sixties, first to do research, then back to Israel for a while, and then finally to take up a post as a lecturer here. Somehow, I found it rather difficult to move on.'

'There are worse places to be.'

'Indeed.' The brown eyes appraised Arnold reflectively. 'And you are one of the Museums and Antiquities people. I've heard your name in several contexts over the years. The *sudarium*. Becket's seal. The Viking sword—'

'I've been lucky.'

Davidson shook his head. 'I never discount the part played by luck in archaeological finds. At the same time, I believe that the luck arrives only after a great deal of hard work. So, I've noted your name over the years — though oddly we've never met before — and admired your work. The academic life has never appealed to you?'

Arnold shook his head. There had been the occasional offer, including a particularly attractive one from California. It would have involved a commitment, professional and personal, that he had not been prepared to make. 'I think I should make it clear that while I have luck and experience, I'm sadly lacking in academic qualifications.'

Davidson laughed aloud. 'Some would say that academic qualifications are only the signs of a misspent youth. Anyway, you've come to talk about the sea cave, I gather.'

'At Abbey Head,' Arnold nodded. 'As you probably know, it was opened only last year. The surprise is that it's reported there are carvings inside the cave, so clearly there's the possibility that there was once an entrance there, open to the beach, but it must have been covered by a rock fall centuries ago. As far as I can make out, there's no written account of its location.'

Davidson drew on his cigarette, nodded sagely. 'Yes, when I heard about its discovery I took a look back through the records. We have documents going back to the fifteenth century in the university archives, and I have my own private collection, but there's no mention of the sea cave. It was opened up now by erosion?'

'The October storms,' Arnold explained. 'There was a considerable landslip. The face of the cliff fell away and the cave was exposed.' He paused. 'The head of the department — Miss Stannard—'

'I've met her, socially.'

'She's negotiated funding for preservation of the cave but there's always the chance that bad weather will affect the site again, so it's important we work quickly. And for that we need all the expertise we can get.'

Davidson spread his hands in deprecation. 'My expertise—'

'Is considerable and well documented. I've read your work: *Sea Caves of Antiquity.*'

Davidson contrived to appear a little embarrassed. 'That was written some years ago now. When I was younger, more enthusiastic — and inclined to flights of rhetoric, I fear.'

'I enjoyed the book.'

'You're not supposed to enjoy an academic treatise,' Davidson chided. 'It denudes a book of its *gravitas.*'

Arnold smiled. 'I don't agree. I see no reason why an academic treatise should not also be readable. Anyway, I came to see you to discuss whether you'd be able to lend us some assistance in the preliminary investigations we'll be making of the site. Thereafter, we'd wish to talk with your department about an ongoing involvement, on your part — for agreed fees, of course — and perhaps by using some of your students for support work.'

Davidson nodded thoughtfully, and took a deep, reflective pull on his cigarette. He watched the blue smoke curl towards the ceiling for a little while. 'I have one or two people who could usefully fit it in with their own research . . . And I'd be delighted, of course, to help out personally. As for a longer term involvement, I'd have to think about that. Things seem to be piling up somewhat, and I'm no longer as young as I was.' He grinned. 'I'm not as adept as I used to be at crawling into narrow places.'

'We've not really started the investigation yet,' Arnold said slowly, 'but it's quite on the cards that the cave was used for ritual purposes.'

'You're baiting a hook, Mr Landon.'

'I know from your book that you're interested in the view that caves were favoured places of natural sanctity, all over the world. And sea caves especially hold a particular place in the imaginations of ancient men.'

Davidson nodded in agreement. He was silent for a little while, and his pouched eyes became vague with old dreams. 'The cycle of birth and death, the tides of the sea,' he murmured, 'the relationship between the living world and that of the chthonic mysteries. Yes . . . you don't need to fish any more, Mr Landon. I'm already hooked. I'll certainly get involved with the Abbey Head investigation. For a while at least, I can't promise it will be long term.'

'Well, I expect to get the Public Works people on the road construction as soon as permission comes through from the owners of Abbey Manor. But there's no reason why a team can't get down and start work on site even while the sea wall is being constructed. What I'll do is—'

There was a light tap on the door. Professor Davidson called out and the door opened. Arnold turned to look back over his shoulder. A young man stood there; curly, unruly, tousled hair, heavy spectacles; open-necked shirt and jeans; urgency and excitement stamped upon his freckled features. 'Ah . . . Professor Davidson? I'm sorry — am I interrupting?'

Davidson hesitated for several seconds. His glance flickered towards Arnold, and quickly away again. It seemed to hold an element of swift calculation. He leaned forward in his chair and beckoned to the young man to enter. 'You rarely pick the most convenient time, Alex, but come on in. Mr Landon, this is Alex Isaacson. One of my research students.'

The young man came forward clumsily, almost tripping as he seemed to rush into the room, extending his hand. Arnold got the impression Alex Isaacson would always blunder into things in his enthusiasm. It would be an endearing, if sometimes irritating characteristic, he guessed.

'Mr Landon works for the Department of Museums and Antiquities. It's opportune that you should appear like this, Alex.'

'I'd heard you were back from Israel, sir. But I didn't get the chance to see you before now. Your diary—'

'Yes, I know,' Davidson replied indulgently. 'There's been much to catch up on. But discussion of your thesis can wait for a moment. Mr Landon is here to talk about work that's about to begin in a sea cave at Abbey Head. I think you might be interested. You might wish to become one of the team. Mr Landon . . . ?'

Arnold launched into an explanation. The young man stood there listening intently, flickers of interest gleaming in his eyes. Davidson leaned back in his chair, squinting through the curling blue smoke of his cigarette, observing the young man as Arnold spoke. When Arnold had finished, Alex Isaacson blurted out, 'That sounds most interesting. Under Professor Davidson's guidance, I've been investigating archaeo-astronomical aspects of cave paintings and petroglyphs — carvings are principally to be found in northern Britain, in Cumbria. I've been concentrating on those located near Langdale, the old stone axe production centre, so it will be fascinating to consider whether art forms in this sea cave have any echoes of the observed links between sea and sky and underworld.'

'Well, we're not sure yet of the extent or nature of the rock art,' Arnold said, trying to rein in a little on the young man's enthusiasm. 'We're informed there is some in the cave, but we'll have to proceed slowly—'

'Ah, well, that suits me,' Isaacson burst in, 'because I have other preoccupations at the moment.'

Davidson was sitting very still in his chair.

'There's no great hurry,' Arnold suggested. 'We have a road to build, a sea wall to construct, and though we'll be starting to work in the cave soon your own contribution would be more important later. A month or so, maybe, and we can talk again about—'

'That would be good,' Isaacson interrupted. 'It would fit in well with my own commitments. Professor Davidson, I have a meeting with the librarian shortly, but I thought I ought to tell you that I've had some exciting news. A contact in Bristol: I'm going down to see him next week.'

Saul Davidson stubbed out his half-finished cigarette. His eyes were hooded. 'Is this about Wenschoff?'

Alex Isaacson nodded, his eyes glittering with excitement. 'I think I'm getting somewhere at last. It's all because of the Americans, you know, their Freedom of Information Act. Everything is so much more open than here. Even so, I didn't think I'd be able to get much, but I've been making enquiries and it turns out there is a lead. A contact in Bristol: an old man in a nursing home. I understand there's information he can give me.'

Davidson was silent for a little while. He spread his hands in almost a helpless gesture. 'I'm not certain you'll be able to find the link you want, Alex—'

'At least it's worth a try!' Alex Isaacson turned to Arnold. 'It's been a sort of obsession, I have to admit. You see, my father was one of the survivors of Auschwitz, the Nazi concentration camp. He's dead now, but though he wouldn't say a great deal about conditions there, he did tell me how he was able to survive because of the assistance he received from one of the guards. A man called Otto Wenschoff. The man was a saint, in my father's eyes. He helped him, gave him food in the late days when the Allied armies were advancing and panic was spreading through the camp guards. You know they began trying to hide what had been going on in the camp? Destroying buildings. Killing inmates. Denial of the horrors of the Nazi regime. But Wenschoff had a conscience. He was like Oskar Schindler. He helped my father — a young boy at the time. He helped him to escape.'

'Alex—' Davidson started to intervene, almost wearily. The young man was not about to stop, now he was properly launched in his enthusiasm. 'You hear so much about the brutalities of that time. The murders. The gas ovens. The hangings. The parades in the snow until men and women dropped. The horrific, insensate inhumanity of that time. But there were also occasional moments, windows of light in the darkness. Otto Wenschoff was one of those. My father told me about it. Talked about how Wenschoff had helped conceal him in the last days. My grandparents died in the camp, but my father escaped. And till the day he died he remembered the man who had saved him. Though he never saw him again.'

Arnold glanced curiously at Saul Davidson. The professor's eyes were averted, as though he was unwilling to listen to the student's story. But then, he had probably heard it many times before.

'My father died about ten years ago now,' Isaacson continued. 'And I had my own life to live. I'm twenty-eight now, and I was rootless, unable to decide on a direction to take, until I came under the influence of Professor Davidson. But some four years ago I also decided to find out what had happened to Otto Wenschoff. Not to meet him, perhaps, though that would have been wonderful, to meet the man who in a way is almost responsible for my existence — I mean, if my father had died in Auschwitz I would not be here today! But to find out what happened to him. To trace his life. To discover whether he died honoured, or in obscurity. To tell the world about him. My search led me to England, and at last to this university where Professor Davidson was able to direct me, give me a road to travel . . .'

Saul Davidson waved his hand in a deprecatory gesture. He reached into his desk, took out another cigarette and lit it. 'I tried to explain to Alex, that he should not become too obsessed with this Wenschoff man. It was a trail that would lead him nowhere. It could divert him from his studies, his career, the need to find a place for himself in the world. The chances of finding out about Wenschoff were remote, and to look back constantly, to trawl over the past, it can be mind-sapping, dangerously so. And, to some extent, I managed to divert him, give him a horizon to look for.'

'And I am grateful for that,' Alex Isaacson said, nodding and smiling. 'But at the same time, I now feel as though I am coming to the end of a long quest. I feel I am near to Otto Wenschoff. My trip to Bristol—'

Saul Davidson interrupted him, turning to Arnold, waving his cigarette. 'My own parents managed to escape the horrors of the Nazis. They were sent to America in 1937. I received my own education in the States, and in Switzerland, and in Israel, before I came here to Newcastle in the late sixties. So I have no painful family memories to dwell upon. But I have been concerned about what Alex is trying to do. I have tried to dissuade him. You see, I have read much about what happened under the Nazis. There is so much we will never be able to understand, particularly those of us who were a persecuted race. It was a time, it seems to me, of great moral dilemmas. Take Oskar Schindler. What was he, in truth? A saint? Or a man who exploited a situation for his own personal profit? There is no doubt one could argue he collaborated with the Nazis. Nor is there any doubt that he saved many Jews. But the motivations, the realities, the balance of the moral dilemmas men like him faced, we will never know.'

'There is no doubt in my mind that Otto Wenschoff saved my father,' Alex Isaacson insisted with a hint of stubbornness.

Professor Davidson smiled. 'I know, Alex. And it should be sufficient to hold the memory of such a man, such an action, in the mind. Many people would argue that the true fact of immortality lies in the reality of memory: as long as you are remembered by one living person after your death, so you remain immortal. But remember also, that if you seek to dredge into the past to discover what motivated a man, what made a man act as he did, you must accept that no man is perfect. We are all flawed. What we do, our ways, they may be the ways of enlightenment — but ultimately they may also be the ways of death.'

Alex Isaacson laughed, an explosion of delight. 'This is why I find my discussions of this matter so stimulating, Professor. It is like a challenge, to prove you wrong. I know that you have a view of humanity which is tinged with cynicism. Perhaps you are right to hold such a view. But I am still convinced that there are some men who are innately human, whatever their circumstances, they have the capacity to rise above them. I believe Otto Wenschoff was such a man. And I believe that when I find him — as I hope to — my confidence will be justified.' He turned to Arnold, shook his hand cordially. 'You will excuse me, I am sure, Mr Landon. I have a meeting with the librarian. I am so sorry to have interrupted your meeting with Professor Davidson. But I really look forward to working with you in due course, at the sea cave. It promises to be a most exciting and rewarding activity.'

He backed out of the room, blundering into a chair as he did so. Then the door closed behind him as he almost ran down the corridor.

'An enthusiastic young man,' Arnold observed wryly.

Saul Davidson stared at him for several seconds, then placed his half-finished cigarette into the ashtray on his littered desk. He sighed despondently. 'I need a drink,' he said and opened the lower drawer of his desk. He placed a bottle of whisky on the desk, pushing aside the litter of papers so that some fluttered to the floor. He ignored them. 'You'll join me, Mr Landon?'

2

During the following week, Arnold finally managed — partly as a result of pressure from Powell Frinton — to get some activity from the Public Works people. Karen Stannard advised him that she had had a call from Daniel Gibbs to say that permission to open up and strengthen the beach road had been given, and he had invited her to dinner to celebrate. During the meal, she informed Arnold, Gibbs had passed her the necessary letter of permission from Hall Gabriel. The sale was going forward, Gibbs claimed to have persuaded Gabriel that the sea cave project was a good thing, and had obtained a letter of agreement from the prospective owner to that effect. Arnold doubted whether Gibbs would have received much in return for his endeavours from Karen Stannard — whatever his hopes and expectations.

The important thing was that clearance had been given: the necessary instructions could then be given and thereafter the work proceeded quickly. Mechanical earthmoving equipment was brought on to the site and the trackway on the headland broadened and flattened within days. A team of men moved in to straighten and construct a retaining wan on the beach road, and within two weeks it proved possible to start bringing moving equipment and machinery down to the beach itself.

Arnold had agreed with the architects of Public Works the plans for the construction of the sea wall. It lay some fifty yards from the narrow entrance to the sea cave itself. Arnold had inspected the site carefully, and it was clear that the building of the wall had to be a priority. The high spring tides could possibly be washing into the cave in a matter of weeks, if something was not done to prevent it. With Karen Stannard, he agreed that it would be best that the inspection team for the cave should be advised that it would not be sensible to commence work until the wall was built. There was simply too much going on at the beach site.

And, to his surprise, Arnold also found his company being sought by Chris Hayman.

It began with Hayman approaching Arnold in the canteen one day, tray in hand, with the diffident request that he be allowed to join Arnold at his table, for lunch. Over the next few days, when Arnold was in the canteen, it became a matter of course. Where previously Hayman had tended to eat alone, now he seemed to seek out Arnold's company. Arnold was not entirely easy with the situation. He felt that he and Chris Hayman really had little in common, but he guessed that the man was lonely, and for the first time in the many years that he had worked in the department, he had found himself someone he could regard as a friend. It was perhaps a misunderstanding of the reason behind Arnold's failing to mention to Karen Stannard the part played by Hayman in the fracas at the Black Horse. It may have been that Hayman wanted to express his gratitude by a display of appreciation and friendship.

Whatever the motivation for the change in behaviour, Hayman not only sought out Arnold, but also became somewhat confessional in his conversation. 'I've tended to feel that I'm different, you know? All these years I've worked in the DMA I've never felt the need for . . . sitting down and talking with someone. But there was my wife, you see. I'd be the last to suggest it was a perfect marriage . . . we never invited people to the cottage, kept very much to ourselves — as you'll have appreciated, she suffered from depression for years, and it wasn't exactly the kind of atmosphere where you could invite people around. But she was there . . . and there was a sort of dependency that meant I neither had time, nor the inclination to develop other relationships.' He wrinkled his brow, thinking back over the way it had been over the years. 'When we married, you know, we had expectations. Somehow, they never came to anything. Loss of the business, her father, dying of his own weaknesses, her mother . . . We lived in a tight little world of our own, now I look back at it. I was tied in, bound into a life which was kind of enclosed.'

Arnold felt sorry for him. Chris Hayman had clearly found difficulty in coming to terms with the loss of his wife. A gaping hole had appeared in his existence, and the only way he could find to plug that gap was to turn to someone who had been there, in the aftermath of his wife's suicide.

Hayman said nothing about the circumstances of his wife's death, other than that he had found her at home that evening, after a long depressive state. 'Overdose of sleeping pills. She'd been collecting them for months. All quite deliberate. It's difficult, you know,' he said, 'coming to terms with something like that. I'm left with the feeling that somehow I failed her.' His brow clouded. 'I did try, try to make things right. All those years ago . . . I tried. But, it all got so involved. So complicated. And now, she's gone, and it's as though it was all a waste, you know what I mean?'

Arnold could not begin to understand, but he did sympathize. Consequently, somewhat against his personal inclinations be found himself being drawn into a relationship that he found occasionally embarrassing, and somewhat wearing. There was something one-dimensional about Chris Hayman: he had concentrated obsessionally upon his marriage and his work, and little else seemed to have intruded upon his consciousness during the last twenty years. Now, with his wife dead, he was introspective, inclined to talk about the past, worry like a dog over a bone over things he felt he had left undone — but there was a vagueness about it all, a disinclination to expose detail. Something still bothered him, Arnold was certain, there was something the man regarded as left undone, a part that was unfinished quite apart from the death of his wife. Arnold suspected it might be due to the general uncertainty of a life suddenly denuded of a central part, a well-organized piece of machinery suddenly breaking down.

'This work you're scheduled to do at the sea cave,' Hayman suddenly said one evening to Arnold, in the pub. He had explained that his car had broken down. Arnold had offered him a lift home to his cottage. On the way, by way of recompense, Hayman had suggested they have a drink together. Sitting in the lounge bar, Hayman suddenly asked a favour. 'I've been spending all these years working away in the department — a clerk, archives, producing report prints, and all that sort of thing — but I've never been *involved*. In the field, I mean. I've never been active at any of the digs, or investigations that the DMA has been responsible for. Office-bound, that's me. Out of things. And it wasn't important, before, it didn't matter. But now . . .'

Arnold could see what was coming and was uncertain how he should react.

'I just find life so difficult, Arnold, with my wife gone. There's a loss, a lack of direction. I just feel I need something new, something different. A new challenge. This sea cave, now . . .'

'It's really a job for experts,' Arnold said uneasily, hoping to head Chris Hayman off without embarrassment. 'I'm pulling a team together—'

'But I hear you're also getting students, people to do the sifting and scraping, that sort of thing. General dogsbody stuff. They're hardly experts. Do you think you could consider me as one of the team? I mean, I'm no expert, I admit, but I could help . . . And it would maybe get me out of this bloody desert I find myself wandering in . . .'

Ruled by sympathy, somewhat against his better judgement, Arnold finally agreed to include Hayman in the group working from the departmental office. He mentioned it casually to Karen Stannard the next morning, in her preoccupation with more important things she raised no objection. Portia Tyrrel had raised an eyebrow when she heard, and muttered something about lame dogs. But Chris Hayman's name had been included.

Arnold thought about it one evening, as he stood on Abbey Head, gazing out to sea, listening to the monotonous roar of the surf a hundred feet below on the beach, when the construction team had gone, and he was alone. Hayman lived not too far from the headland. His evenings were lonely, his days unrewarding. Arnold could understand the man needed a new challenge, to get away from the past. He'd wanted to gain an opportunity to forget a way of life.

As Professor Saul Davidson had seemed to want Alex Isaacson to forget the past, two weeks ago when he had talked to Arnold in his university office.

* * *

Arnold had accepted the generous glass of whisky offered him, and leaned back in his chair. Saul Davidson seemed suddenly despondent, his brow furrowed, lines of disappointment around his mouth. He took a sip of his whisky, then glowered at the amber liquid in his glass. 'You weren't around here in the seventies,' he said, almost accusingly.

Arnold shook his head. 'I was living in Yorkshire then.'

He still had golden memories of that time. There had been long walks with his father in the dales when they had inspected Roman smelting furnaces, climbed the fells, sought out long-decayed lead mines, inspected twisted, rusting remains of old machinery, looked at the industrial heritage left to them by men of another time. He remembered how his father had taught him, given him a feeling for wood, the ancient timbers of a medieval barn, tie beams and pendants, wall plates and mountants. They had looked at old buildings together. His father had explained how the old master masons had learned by trial and error, how even shafts and mouldings had been executed with the axe, before bolsters came to be used — and how the bolster marks, the 'toolings' on stone, could be so neatly aligned as to make the stone appear to have been machined. He had learned of massive stone roofs pinned with chicken bones, and of the carving with iron claws of slender, soaring pillars reaching to cathedral heights.

'I'm older than you,' Davidson said gloomily, sipping at his whisky and squinting through the thickening cigarette smoke haze. 'I remember the Six Day War when Israel occupied Jerusalem, the West Bank, Gaza and the Golan Heights. It was just before I came to England and it's easy to forget now what England was like at that time. Six million working days lost to strikes in 1970; postal workers' strike in 1971; miners' strike in 1972. Militancy, flying pickets, student riots in support of the workers, and then the Arab-Israeli war in 1973. It was twenty-five years after the end of the Nazis but the world was still in turmoil. The IRA and Bloody Sunday in 1972, terrorist bombs on the British mainland at the Old Bailey and Scotland Yard, at the Boat Show and the Tower of London. Pro-IRA, pro-Palestinian Arabs, Angry Brigade anarchists . . . you look back now, and you wonder what it was all about? Had we learned nothing from the past? But at the time . . .'

He was silent for a little while, sipping at his whisky.

Arnold waited, slightly uneasy, not knowing where the reminiscences were taking them.

'I'd been protected from the worst effects of Nazism, by the fact that my parents were relatively well off, and had fled Germany before the outbreak of war,' Davidson continued moodily. 'And I'd decided on a university career. But somehow, all around there were problems. The world had not lost its capacity for senseless rage, and even here in Newcastle there were reverberations of the past. There seemed no sense of social justice: there was the feeling that violence was necessary to achieve political aims, and students took to the streets, police were attacked, it seemed that law and order was in danger of collapse. What was one to do in such circumstances?'

'You were a young lecturer then,' Arnold said after a short silence.

Saul Davidson nodded. 'Young, and maybe with a sense of mission, I suppose. I got involved with politics — didn't everyone? I was not much older than my students, and when they marched . . . But it all got ugly. Violent. I remember the rioting in support of the miners. The students were howling about police brutality. There were several of my own students heavily involved. For some, it cost them their futures, in a sense. They dropped out, concentrating on anarchic pursuits. Others settled down, but did not return to their university courses. A strange time: students, workers, anarchists, fascists, communists, all struggling in the streets. Ultimately, for what?'

Arnold sipped his whisky. It was a good malt. Saul Davidson had never lost the taste for the good life, he guessed. 'The times have moved on,' he said quietly. . .

'Yes,' Davidson sighed, 'but the past has a way of rising up in front of your eyes, time and time again.'

'Alex Isaacson?' Arnold hazarded.

Davidson hesitated, then nodded sombrely. 'I have tried to warn him. When he first came to me and mentioned his . . . odyssey, I tried to laugh it away. But he's obsessed with a romantic dream, and what he sees as a search for the truth. The trouble is that truth is not a single pillar: it can be multi-faceted. It's what men see in their minds and hearts, and interpretations can differ. That was the problem in the sixties and seventies, interpretations differed. And people were hurt.'

'How can Alex Isaacson be hurt by seeking the man who saved his father?' Arnold asked curiously.

'Because Otto Wenschoff might not have been the man Alex thinks he was,' Davidson replied bluntly.

There was a short silence. At last, Arnold asked, 'How do you mean?'

Saul Davidson finished his drink, poured himself another, glanced at Arnold, who shook his head. He was beginning to feel that Davidson was heading for a stiff drinking session, dealing with a need fuelled by the past, and he had no desire to join in. But he was curious.

'It's like I said to Alex here in this room,' Davidson went on. 'The men who were involved in those camps — Auschwitz, Belsen, Treblinka and the rest — whether as prisoners or jailers, they were living their lives almost in a moral vacuum where nothing was normal, there were no rules, nothing was sacrosanct, not even human life. And although humanity and compassion occasionally gleamed through the murk of terror, so they could be swamped again by the needs of the hour, the demands of the system, the obligations of office perhaps, or the individual need to survive. Did you know that there were Jewish police squads, enforcing the Nazi rule in the camps? For God's sake, supervising, and enforcing the destruction of their own people!'

Arnold was silent for a while. He felt unable to pass comment on a past that was felt so personally by the man facing him. 'You're suggesting that Alex might learn more than is good for him.'

Davidson shrugged. 'The loss of innocence. The ways of death.'

'I don't understand.'

Davidson poured himself another whisky. 'The violence of the seventies, the student riots, the bombs, the air of impending doom — it all threw up something else. The search for scapegoats, the digging up of the past. It was years since the Nuremberg hearings, but the search for Nazi war criminals was still going on. And there were stories that a number of them had managed to escape the judgements that awaited them. We all heard the stories of those who escaped to Brazil, Chile, other South American republics. We all read about Nazi gold, priceless art treasures, the huge financial support that leading Nazis obtained, to develop new identities and careers for themselves in post-war Europe and the New World. But what of all the others, the small men, the men with names not so notorious, who slipped through the nets cast for them in the chaos that was the defeated Germany? They were sometimes Poles, or Romanians, Serbs or Russians, not German nationals. But they had fought for Germany. They had served in the SS, worked in the labour camps; they had killed in Auschwitz and Belsen and Riga.' He glowered at his glass. 'Otto Wenschoff was Romanian.'

'I had read that many of the camp guards were nationalities other than German.'

'And in the absolute turmoil that was post-war Europe many of them managed to come into France, and Holland . . . and England. They made their way silently across Europe, after the war. They changed their names, managed to escape scrutiny with false papers, wiped out their pasts, settled down to lead respectable lives, got decent jobs, expected, after a while, to remain in obscurity.' He grunted, sipped at his whisky, then lit another cigarette. 'But always there was the searching.' He waved his cigarette, watching its parabolic glowing end. 'I wonder whether it'll be the alcohol, or tobacco which will get me in the end?'

'What do you know about this Otto Wenschoff?' Arnold asked.

'You mean what do I know about Otto Wenschoff that I have not told Alex Isaacson?' Davidson took a deep breath. 'Maybe I should have told him. Instead, hoping to save his dreams, his naïve view of the essential goodness of man, his belief in humanity, I just tried to steer him away from seeking out this man. You see, Mr Landon, here is the paradox. Alex Isaacson's father told his son about this great saviour, the humanitarian, the man who had stood out against the system, who had risked his own life to save a boy caught up in the inhumanity of Auschwitz, But others tell of another Otto Wenschoff. A brute. A murderer. A killer, who treated people like animals. There is the moral dilemma I spoke of earlier. How can one decide what is the truth, in a sink like Auschwitz? I've been there, you know. It's just a series of barrack blocks . . . so bloody *ordinary*! But it saw scenes of depravity. And sometimes, compassion. But if a man degrades human beings, murders women and children, is he later to be lauded for saving a young boy, one of many whom he otherwise treated like cattle?'

'Do you have proof of this?' Arnold asked. 'Do you know that Wenschoff was . . .'

'A monster?' Davidson laughed bleakly. 'Proof . . . maybe not, but I'm pretty sure, as others have been certain. I tell you, there were stories . . . and they were here in the north-east of England. You see, in the middle of all those riots, and battles in the streets, and bombs in the pubs, there was also a hunt going on. For the man called Otto Wenschoff. He had been traced to England; it was said he had buried himself in obscurity in Newcastle. He had finally got a job on the railway network. He had ended up living quietly as a railway worker. And he had changed his name.'

'Are you saying he was actually *traced* here?'

'That's right. I have it on good authority. There was a police investigation. Otto Wenschoff had come to England with forged papers. He called himself Arthur Winder. He was living at Fenham, working as a platelayer.'

'But why haven't you told this to Isaacson?' Arnold asked, puzzled.

Davidson shrugged. 'What was the point? He has his dreams. If the reality is that Otto Wenschoff was a depraved monster. If the truth is that Otto Wenschoff was indeed Arthur Winder, a man who had escaped the consequences of his crimes, what was to be gained by my telling Alex?'

'Do you mean you can't be certain that Wenschoff was this person, Arthur Winder?'

'It was never proved.'

'Why?'

'Because the trail went cold. In 1972, Arthur Winder just disappeared.' Saul Davidson frowned, sighed, stubbed out his cigarette in a hard, jabbing motion. 'It's as though the man vanished, right off the face of the earth.'

3

Karen Stannard was able to use her relationship with Daniel Gibbs to good effect immediately upon hearing that the time was ripe for work to begin at the sea cave. She called Arnold into her office to explain.

'The project papers you prepared have now been sent over my signature to London,' she explained crisply, 'and I've received a phone call to say that the appropriate funding will be made available within weeks. The Public Works people have been active?'

'They have,' Arnold nodded. 'The beach road has been constructed, they've moved heavy machinery down to the site and the sea wall should be finished by the end of the week.'

'Which means we can get started on the investigation itself.' Her tone signified a satisfied approval. It was something he rarely heard in her voice. 'Fine. I've now been in touch with Daniel Gibbs and he's agreed that we should have a launch of the whole Landslip activity at Abbey Manor itself. He's discussed it with Hall Gabriel, who will be the new owner by that time, and they've agreed to hold a press conference at the manor. Gibbs and Gabriel will be there; I shall introduce the scheme; we'll pay a visit down to the site, and all the local media will be contacted. I've handed over the marketing of Landslip to our PR people, and they assure me we'll get excellent support, including television.'

'Isn't this going somewhat over the top?' Arnold queried.

'Nonsense,' she flashed. 'Don't be so stick-in-the-mud. This is an opportunity to project a bright new image for the department. I've always felt under previous management that we never seemed to trumpet our skills and successes sufficiently. I intend to remedy that. So, we'll have press and television, we'll have the use of the manor house, Mr Gabriel is apparently prepared to lay on drinks and light refreshments, and when we reach the site I'll want the team assembled to take part in a photo opportunity. That's where you come in: I want a brochure prepared, providing details of the team we're using, ready for handing out to the press, and for general use for visitors to the site thereafter. I'm hoping to persuade Mr Gabriel that we should be allowed to erect a small information centre near the public right of way on the clifftop itself. He hasn't demurred, so far.'

Arnold nodded. She was going great guns for this, he thought. Arrival of the Queen of Sheba — Karen Stannard making her mark as the new head of the Department of Museums and Antiquities.

'You've got your team together?'

'I've already supplied you with a list.'

She frowned thoughtfully. 'Ah, yes . . . just one thing about that. I took another look at it. You've included one of our archives staff — Chris Hayman. Not exactly his line of work, over the years, is it?'

'We need workers. He's interested. And it'll help give him a new challenge.'

'Help him get over the loss of his wife, you mean.' Karen stared thoughtfully at Arnold for a little while. 'You're too soft, you know, Arnold. One of these days it will be your undoing. You sure he really can help?'

'I think we should let him have the opportunity,' Arnold replied stubbornly. 'And then, as far as the team is concerned, if we're to have all this publicity, maybe we should make another addition.'

Her eyes flickered a suspicious glance towards his. There was a dark green depth to them today, he thought, signs of a possible storm. 'Who?'

'Portia Tyrrel.'

'Why?'

'She's photogenic.'

There was a long silence. Karen Stannard leaned back in her chair, regarding Arnold thoughtfully. She picked up a pencil, began to play with it between her fingers. Somewhere in the room a fly droned monotonously. 'You know, Arnold, I've had the feeling, recently, that you and Portia have become somewhat . . . close.'

'I don't know what that's supposed to mean. We're colleagues. As you and I are.'

'Not quite that,' she purred with an edge of malice in her tone. 'Whisperings in corners, that sort of thing. Far be it for me to suggest that you're having some sort of relationship with my assistant, outside working hours. But . . . are you?'

'No.' His mind flickered back to the sunny afternoon, on the moor some months ago. He closed the image down, slamming a shutter on the past. 'It's just as I said. If you're going to have a photo opportunity at the site, I think it would make good sense to allow her to do the presentation. Look better on television.'

'I'd expected you to do it.'

'I don't see myself as a TV presenter. We'd get more mileage if she appeared.'

'I could do it,' Karen muttered, her eyes flaring slightly at his stubbornness.

'But then it would look like a one-woman show. You're already scheduling yourself to do the presentation at Abbey Manor. You'll be fronting for the department at the press conference. If you take over at the site itself, maybe people will think you're developing . . .'

'*Folie de grandeur*?' she asked frostily. But as he saw the shifting colours in her eyes, he guessed she was perceptive enough to take his point.

* * *

The day itself proved to be inauspicious. The weather forecast for the previous twenty-four hours had been gloomy and for once proved accurate. Overnight, strong winds built up and roofs were rattled and stripped from County Durham down into Yorkshire. The winds had died down only slightly by morning, dark clouds piled up in the east, and the rain began to fall steadily. By midday the skies had lightened somewhat, but when Arnold drove to Abbey Head just before lunchtime the wind was shifting and there was a dark purple bruising in the western sky that suggested the storm had not yet blown itself out.

A number of cars had already parked at the headland itself, and television crews were assembling their gear at Abbey Manor. Arnold found difficulty in parking: a certain area had been marked off for officials, but it was full. In the end he managed to pull in under the dripping beech trees to one side of the gravel drive, and consequently arrived somewhat damply at the manor house.

Karen Stannard emerged from a milling crowd in the library and looked him up and down, with a certain contempt. 'You look bedraggled,' she accused. She, on the other hand, looked as beautiful as usual. She had swept back her hair, leaving a light fringe to frame her features, emphasizing the fine bone structure, and highlighting her magnificent eyes. If she was dressed with a certain formality, the dark suit nevertheless served only to highlight her femininity, figure-hugging, outlining the perfection of her slim-hipped, firm-bosomed form. She was at her best socially, moving with ease between dignitaries from the council and representatives of Northern Heritage, chatting with the television crews, exchanging jokes with newspaper reporters, posing for a photograph for social

78

magazines and professional publications in the archaeology field. He listened as she gave several interviews, off the cuff, confident, radiant in her professionalism. The alcohol was dispensed freely about the room, and the sound levels rose.

Daniel Gibbs was looking pleased with himself. 'He's staying as close as he dares to the Goddess herself,' Portia Tyrrel whispered to Arnold, as Karen Stannard eyed them warily. Hall Gabriel also moved among the press and visiting councillors, confident, charming, well-experienced at this kind of entertainment. This was his home, his scene, his milieu: Arnold overheard him explaining to one reporter that for him this was a homecoming, the local boy makes good story, the return of the humble lad of yesteryear to take over the house he had dreamed of all those years ago.

Within the wheeling, chattering, noisily imbibing group of people enjoying themselves in the free hospitality of Abbey Manor, two people only seemed ill at ease. Sean Corman circulated, but seemed to say very little, and his eyes were constantly wary, as though seeking trouble. He remained relatively close to Gabriel, who largely ignored him, but Corman exuded an edgy watchful control, as though at any moment he was expecting an intrusion of terrorists.

Arnold said so to Portia.

'Looking at the amount of alcohol being consumed, I would suggest it might be an *infusion* rather than intrusion,' she murmured before whispering away in her high-necked silk shantung dress, providing the northern journalists with hints of Eastern promise.

The other man seemingly out of place was Chris Hayman. He had been reluctant to even come to the manor house: 'It's just not my scene,' he had muttered, when Arnold had told him his presence was expected. 'I'm not a social animal — never have been.' He had eventually been persuaded to attend, but he remained in one corner of the room, shabby-suited, back to the wall, an untouched drink in his hands, his expression blank, but his body language expressing his desire to be anywhere but here.

Arnold could understand it to a certain extent. Hayman's life had changed so significantly with the suicide of his wife that coming to terms with a gathering of this nature could be unnerving for him. Arnold felt he should spend some time with him, but was guiltily reluctant to do so. He had the feeling he might get trapped in the corner by Hayman's insecurity and unease, a straw grasped by a man drowning in unfamiliar society. The moment passed, however, as there was a call for silence. Hall Gabriel, Daniel Gibbs, Powell Frinton and an assorted group of dignitaries involved — or semi-involved — in the Landslip Project were called, and assembled at the far end of the room for Karen Stannard to make a short address.

She spoke well, her tone modulated, almost sensual, with, when her formula pleasantries called for it, an occasional deep, throaty chuckle that Arnold could see sent shivers of pleasure up and down a number of male spines. She made the appropriate announcements, gave thanks to individuals by name, and outlined briefly and succinctly the aims of the project, the activities that were to be undertaken at the site, and the expectations of the department as to what was to be found in the sea cave. The applause that came at the end of her speech was warm, well meant, and appreciative.

The Queen of Sheba had certainly arrived.

After her brief speech the circulatory drinking continued for a while until, checking his watch, Arnold realized he'd better get down to the beach site. He nodded to Hayman, collected Portia and the three of them used Arnold's car to drive down the newly constructed track to the beach. During the brief ride Hayman seemed tense, preoccupied: he had clearly not enjoyed the company at Abbey Manor.

Arnold parked the car near the sea wall. A buffeting breeze was coming in from the sea. An awning had been erected near the entrance to the sea cave, but it was fluttering wildly in the fierce wind and Arnold feared that at any moment it might get blown away.

'I don't think there's going to be much chance of getting decent photographs down here today,' he suggested to Portia as the rest of the team huddled under the fluttering awning. 'If Karen's got any sense, she'll call off this little session.'

She did not. In a little while they began to troop down, a small shuttle bus bringing a group of media people down to the site. It was raining again, heavily, and no one seemed particularly happy as they clustered together under the awning, and the rain hammered on the canvas.

Karen Stannard glared at Arnold as though this were all his fault. 'I can hardly hear myself think!' she called.

'It doesn't look as though it's going to let up,' Arnold replied. 'There's no sign of the television crew — I think they've got more sense than to come down.'

Angrily, Karen snapped, 'Well, at least get some of these other photographers organized, with the cave entrance behind the team.'

Arnold did as she ordered. He spoke to the cameramen, organized the damp, miserable huddled group briefly in front of the cave entrance, and once shutters had been hurriedly clicked everyone began to depart. Karen Stannard went back with the shuttle bus. As the rest of the team began to make their way up the beach track Arnold, Portia and Chris Hayman were left alone under the awning. Portia grimaced, as she looked around her. 'Shouldn't we take this down, before it blows away?'

Arnold shook his head. 'The Public Works team'll be down to dismantle it shortly. But I'll have to wait here until they arrive.'

'Which means we're stuck here too, if we want a lift back up the hill.' She put her head out of the shelter briefly, inspecting the driving rain. 'I'm sure this is going to blow the awning away any moment. Don't you think we'd be safer in the cave? I haven't even seen inside it yet.'

Before Arnold could reply, she darted out of the shelter of the awning, silk shantung dress gleaming under the raincoat thrown loosely about her, and ran across to the cave entrance, stooping to avoid the overhanging rock.

Cursing under his breath, Arnold followed; reluctantly, it seemed, Chris Hayman came along behind.

The cave entrance was narrow, a cleft in the rock that had been opened by erosion and falling shale. Portia was standing just inside the entrance, peering inwards. 'Bloody dark in here. But I fancy I can see . . . Have you got a light, Arnold?'

The rain lashed down outside. Arnold cursed again, huddled under his raincoat and ran back to the car. He retrieved a flashlight from the glove compartment and ran back to the cave entrance. Hayman was standing just inside. Portia had ventured further inwards and as he scrambled through the fissure to join her she beckoned, held out her hand for the torch.

A few feet from the entrance the cave widened from a natural subterranean passage to what seemed a four-lobed chamber, its roof rising to above ten feet in height. Portia flashed the torch about her, flickering the beam along the wall, and faded, ancient images emerged. The floor was littered with shells, crunching under their feet; pieces of quartz glittered in the walls, naturally embedded or placed there by human hands Arnold could not yet make out. Oddly enough, ahead of them a faint natural light glowed.

Portia led the way as they moved deeper into the sea cave, the torchlight flickering over illusory images, configurations in the shiny, dripping rock, traces of pigment, simulacra, an animal, an attenuated human figure in flight, configurations of clouds and fire. Arnold felt a sudden cold shiver against his spine: this had been a sacred place for millennia. He was reminded of the words the Greeks had to describe the concept of space in such a location — *topos*, meaning the physical aspects, and *chora*, the mysterious, less passive property of space. He felt it about him, the subtle, poetic quality that provokes the sensibilities. This is why men would have come here, perhaps made ritual deposits here, felt the world soul, the *anima mundi*, emerge here.

'How did they get in to do all this work?' Portia's voice echoed in the depths of the cave, skittering against the roof, and suddenly she extinguished the torch. After a few

moments, as their eyes grew accustomed to the sudden darkness the faint, suffusive glow became apparent, and Arnold
could make out the dim form of Portia standing ahead of
him. She seemed ethereal, bathed in a faint bluish light that
touched her from above. She stood still, head back, eyes seeking the roof. 'How did they get in?' she asked again, almost
reverently.

Arnold moved closer to her. 'My guess is that there was
once an entrance near where we came in — maybe even the
same entrance. But at some stage there would have been a
shifting of the rock, a fall of the cliff face, and the entrance
would have been buried and closed, possibly for thousands
of years. Who knows? What is certain, is that our ancestors
used this cave, saw it as a sacred place. We've seen some
evidence . . .'

'But there's also the evidence of our senses,' Portia
breathed in subdued excitement. 'Can't you feel it, Arnold?
There's a sort of numinous feel about it, a presence, something beyond the natural.'

Arnold knew what she meant. Behind him, he could
hear the steady, harsh breathing of Chris Hayman, almost
invisible in the dimness. Arnold wondered whether he too
was aware of the impression that here was the entrance to
the underworld, the *tirtha* of the Hindu religion, the crossing
place; the *samsara*, the ceaseless river-like flow of birth and
death and birth again. The sea cave encapsulated what men
across the world had felt in similar holy places: reverence,
awe, sanctity and mystery.

'And this light . . .' Portia exclaimed softly.

The bluish glow from the rock above outlined her head
eerily. Arnold could make out her features, the slanting line
of her cheekbones, the deep hollows of her eyes. He looked
up and could see that the light emerged high above their
heads, angling in from the outside world, faded, but real.
'It must be a fissure in the cliff face, high above the beach,'
Arnold suggested. 'It's slanting in . . . one can imagine how
it would have felt in here, in primitive societies.'

Portia shivered suddenly, almost as though she had been touched by the same thoughts that Arnold had experienced earlier. 'This place . . . it's special. It's as though this is where the gods would have lived . . .'

Then she screamed.

It had begun with what seemed to be a slight movement in the air, the touch of a whispering breath on their cheeks. The sensation was unnerving but it was followed instantly by a sharp cracking sound, a sudden rumble, and Portia screamed, dropping the torch and clutching at Arnold in sudden panic. As the rumbling spread around them, growing in intensity, Arnold scrabbled for the torch among the broken shells on the floor of the cave. He felt something else there, hard, brittle, smooth, and as he gratefully grasped at the torch and flicked it back on he realized that the floor of the cave was also littered with small, shattered bone fragments.

He dragged Portia back towards the entrance of the sea cave, aware that Hayman was tumbling out ahead of him, but she resisted him, panicked, gripping his hand fiercely as the rumbling grew to a roar, ending with a final crashing sound and a cloud of choking dust. Then, as they both leaned against the wall, Portia shivering in his arms, the noise receded and died, and a dust-laden silence swept in about them. Hayman shouted from the cave entrance. Arnold called back to reassure him they were unhurt, but neither he nor Portia now seemed to want to leave the depths of the sea cave. The dust was settling about them and slowly, as the air cleared, the soft bluish light came back again, like a benison.

They stood there, Portia nestling close to him, shivering slightly, and they waited as though expecting the spirit of the place to emerge, to envelop them. Arnold felt no surge of fear, rather it was a sense of inevitability, as though it had all happened before, a million times, when the dark earth rose to bring them to its heart, and silence was the only sound.

After a little while, as the blue glow touched and held them Portia moved, raised her face to his. 'What happened?'

He could feel the warmth of her, pressed against him, and the faint image of the sun-touched fell came to him again, when they had last been close like this. He pulled his thoughts back from that brink. 'A rock fall,' he suggested.

She gave a nervous, giggling sound. 'I thought . . . it was as though the gods of my ancestors . . . my Chinese mother used to tell me tales . . .'

'A rock fall,' Arnold reassured her. 'That noise, the dust . . .' He raised the torch, sent the flickering beam above his head, inspecting the rock, then ahead, deeper into the cave. 'You see, above our heads there's been no movement. The fall is down there, in the depths of the chamber. Come . . .'

He moved away from her, curious. After a slight hesitation, she followed him. Behind them, Hayman called out, 'What's going on? What's happening?'

'It's okay. We're all right. There's been a fall.'

It was at the far end of the cave. The bluish glow was behind them. Ahead, the air seemed somewhat cooler, fresher, and there was a hint of dampness, ancient odours in their nostrils. The smooth walls of the cave glistened under the torchlight, and more faded images leapt out at them, but Arnold was peering forward to the far end of the chamber. 'There,' he said, pointing. 'That's where the fall was. But there's something odd about it the way the roof curves at that point.'

He moved forward, flashing the torch. He saw the pile of broken rock, the rubble, and what seemed a deposit of rubbish. He leaned forward, stretched out his hand among the littered stones, and touched something smooth. He picked it up, inspected it in the torchlight.

'What have you got?' Portia asked, coming close behind him.

'It's a piece of horn,' Arnold replied. 'Carved. An earth mother, heavy belly, sagging breasts. It's a votive offering.'

'Let me see!' she exclaimed in excitement. Arnold handed it to her, shining the torch on it briefly, then swung back to the pile of rocks in front of him. Something glittered faintly, caught in the sharp light. Arnold leaned forward, teased it out of the rocks, feeling the harshness of rust under his fingers. Puzzled, he picked it up, rubbing his fingers over rusted metal.

'What's that?'

Portia's voice was eerie, sending a dying echo to the rocks above them, fluttering down again into the cave chamber.

'It's a piece of metal . . .'

'What sort? Old?'

'It's a disc, I think,' Arnold said slowly, turning it over in his fingers. He peered at it inspecting it carefully in the torchlight. 'A piece of it snapped off. But there's something engraved on it.'

'Can you make it out? Glyphs? Ornamental carving? Prehistoric, or Viking?'

'No.' Arnold shook his head slowly. 'It's a thin piece of tin, it seems, and there's lettering on it. Three letters, to be precise.' He was silent for a while.

'So, tell me,' Portia demanded urgently.

'I think the letters are L, N and E.'

'What do you think they stand for?' Portia asked wonderingly.

CHAPTER THREE

1

'London and North Eastern,' Culpeper rumbled. 'The old LNER. It's an identity disc belonging to someone who worked on the railway. It's got a number stamped on the back.'

'Are you able to identify the owner?' Arnold Landon asked.

Culpeper squinted thoughtfully out of the window of his office at Ponteland. There was a bunch of starlings squabbling in the trees across the manicured lawn below. They had become very common birds in gardens, he'd heard. 'We're working at it. How do you reckon he came to be in that cave?'

Arnold shrugged. 'When I picked up that disc, and realized there were human bones scattered nearby, and remains of old, rotting clothing, I was puzzled. I mean, the sea cave had been sealed for millennia, and yet there were the remains of a modern man there. Then I realized it would have had something to do with the rock fall.'

Culpeper nodded. He had visited the cave with Farnsby. Forensic had bagged up and taken away a considerable pile of bones. The next step was to sort them properly, but also to take a closer look at the rock pile itself. 'We got a lot of stuff out of that cave. Stuff of more interest to you than us, is my guess. Artefacts, animal bones — and the remains of someone who worked on the railway more than a few years ago.'

Landon was frowning, as though he was churning something over in his mind. But he said nothing. After a little while, Culpeper grunted. 'All right, I've read your statement, you've signed it . . . but you talk about facts only. No suppositions.'

'I thought that's the way you would want it,' Landon replied. 'Details of what we did that day, how we went into the sea cave, the rock fall and the manner in which we stumbled across the bones.'

'It is what I wanted,' Culpeper agreed. 'But now I'd like something more. Your thoughts about it all. How do you think those bones, and the disc, got in the cave?'

Arnold Landon took a deep breath. 'I've thought about it a great deal. This coastline, that headland, over the centuries it's taken a lot of pounding by wind, rain, the sea. The cave would probably have been open at one time, and that would have been when ancient men worked on those walls, carved those simulacra, painted those designs. But then the cliff would have been eroded, rock would have crashed down, sealing the cave for hundreds, maybe thousands of years. The sacred place was closed: that's the way ancient man would have seen it. But there was another place on Abbey Head. It's a rock fissure, some distance back from the cliff edge. It's known locally as Hades Gate.'

'The entrance to hell.'

'More accurately, to the underworld,' Arnold Landon suggested. 'The fissure, it too was a sacred place, from all I've been able to ascertain, and with the sea cave closed I think it took on even greater significance. I was talking with Daniel Gibbs, the previous owner of the manor house, and he told me that as a child he used to be scared by strange noises coming out of the fissure up there on the headland. I've discussed it since with Professor Davidson, at the university—'

'Saul Davidson?' Culpeper interrupted.

Landon nodded. 'That's right. He's an expert on ritual sea caves. He managed to find some references to Hades Gate, going back a century and more. It seems the idea of mysterious sounds, voices, wailing is not new. That fissure has had a reputation for linking the spirit world with living men for a very long time. Men believed that the cleft in the headland spoke. It became a ritual centre, that's my guess, because it was seen as a spirit place.'

'It *spoke*.' Culpeper could not keep the disbelief out of his tone.

Landon nodded. 'I've thought a lot about it. You've been in the cave now, Mr Culpeper. You'll no doubt have noticed there's an odd bluish light in the chamber. It's the result of another fissure in the cliff face that leads into the cave roof, a sort of blow-hole, if you know what I mean.'

'Go on.'

'Within the cave, the blow-hole provides a certain amount of diffused light. Gives the place an eerie, supernatural feel. I can imagine it would have been one of the contributory factors, centuries ago, that gave the cave a supernatural ambience. But with the wind in the right direction, that fissure could also set up a moaning sound, a whistling, a wailing.' He paused, considering. 'It's my guess that if we had investigated the deeper recesses of that cave before the rock fall, we might have discovered that the back section of the chamber wasn't solid rock. I think there may have been a sort of narrow chimney there, leading up to Hades Gate. Centuries ago, after the sea cave was closed, sounds must have begun to come up through the fissure on the headland. I think the sounds were made by the wind whining through that blow-hole, and echoing up the shaft, the chimney, the fissure that led up to the headland itself. It led people to believe spirits dwelt there. They started to use Hades Gate as a ritual site: a vulvic opening into which they would throw votive offerings to Mother Earth, or Gaia, or the gods of the underworld — whatever their particular beliefs might have been. And it spoke to them, and their shamans would have interpreted the words for them.'

There was a short silence as Landon stared at the unmoved Culpeper. 'That's what I think. When you've finished there, Mr Culpeper, and my team can start work there, I think we'll find a great deal more relating to our ancient past.'

'And our railwayman?'

Landon shrugged. 'He could have been wandering up there on the headland, in the dark, or on a windy night, lost his footing, slipped into the crevice. One can only hope that he would have died quickly. If he had lain long in the fissure, unable to get out or attract help, it could have been a slow death.'

'And his calls for help . . .'

'If heard at all, would have been dismissed perhaps, by local people, as a phenomenon they knew about. As I've explained, Hades Gate had a reputation for mysterious wailings.'

Culpeper sniffed. A sealed cave with ancient remains. A blow-hole in the cliff causing echoing sounds up a natural shaft to the clifftop. 'So you think that rock fall you experienced, it closed the bottom of the shaft?'

'That's about it. The storms over the last weeks, the heavy rain — I think it caused a landslide within Hades Gate itself. Unhappily, it occurred when we were in the sea cave below — it scared the hell out of us. And the collapse brought down the railwayman's bones, from where they have probably been lying in the chimney for a long time. His bones, and other, older material. It's all a series of coincidences. The remains of this railwayman, they might never have been found . . .' He was silent for a little while. 'Can you give me any idea of when we're to be allowed to return to the cave? We have work to do there.'

Culpeper shrugged. 'It shouldn't be too long. I want the forensic report on the bones we've found, but I don't think there's a great deal for us to do after that. As far as we can ascertain, the remains of the rotted clothing, the state of the bones themselves, the disc you found, it all suggests something that happened a long time ago. And it's all likely

91

to have been the result of an accident, many years ago. We've got plenty of other things to do . . . so it shouldn't be too long before you can get back in there and start sifting through ancient dust, if that's what turns you on . . .'

Yet after Landon had left the office, Culpeper was still left with an uneasy feeling in his stomach. Something Landon had said had started a train of thought, briefly. Train of thought. Railwaymen. He had the suspicion he was missing something. But he thrust the thought aside, and wandered into the corridor, making his way to the office where Detective Inspector Farnsby worked.

'So how you getting on?' he asked.

'With which matter, sir?' There was a sour note in Farnsby's voice. He was clearly somewhat annoyed by the workload Culpeper had given him. Culpeper enjoyed that. There was nothing he liked better than getting under Farnsby's skin. And he had not too many weeks left to enjoy that sensation, with retirement looming.

'Well, let's take the thing I've just been discussing with Landon. The business at the sea cave.'

'I don't know why we're bothering, sir.' Farnsby's lean, dissatisfied features were marked with scorn. 'I mean, a skeleton that's at least twenty years old — maybe more? We've no chance of discovering what caused the death it might have been an accident, or suicide, and it was all so long ago, what's the point?'

'Keeping things tidy, that's the point,' Culpeper replied cheerfully. 'Anyway, as I asked . . .'

Farnsby lifted a surly shoulder. 'I've got an enquiry out into the local records for the LNER. They're still held in Newcastle — lodged in the archives in the library.'

'Thank God for railway enthusiasts.'

'It's possible we'll come up with a check on the number of the identity disc. *Possible*. But that's the only lead we have at the moment.'

'Let me know when the information comes in. And the other matter I asked you to deal with?'

Farnsby took a deep, irritated breath. 'Alex Isaacson. The young girl who came to see you. We're working on it.' He did not add, *reluctantly*.

It had been a matter of chance, really. She had wandered into Ponteland HQ, a bonny-looking lass, and Culpeper had been in a grandfatherly kind of good humour, and she seemed a bit lost, so he'd asked her if she needed help. She did. It was not Culpeper's usual way, but he had warmed to her and when she told him she'd lost a friend of hers he took her into the canteen, bought her a cup of tea and asked her all about it.

'It's not that he's sort of my boyfriend, if you know what I mean. We're good mates, sort of . . . He's quite a bit older than me, research student you see, while I'm only in my second year of a sociology degree, but as soon as he took a room in the house in Victoria Terrace where there's a bunch of students staying, we kind of hit it off, you know what I mean? He wasn't like the others, you know, booze, fags, try to get into your knickers. He was serious. And he had interesting things to talk about.'

'Such as?' Culpeper had asked indulgently.

'Well, you know, the war and all that. *Ancient* stuff. He's Jewish, you see, and he was very interested in everything about the war, and particularly the concentration camps because some of his family died there. And he'd developed this kind of mission: it was exciting, really, and so *romantic*. They have this kind of deal going in Israel, honouring people who had saved Jews, they set up a kind of remembrance, like they did for Schindler . . . I saw that film. *Scary*. Alex — that's his name, Alex Isaacson — he admitted he didn't think he could swing that sort of deal for the man he was trying to trace, but it was his mission, even so. He had been told, sort of family tradition, that this guard at Auschwitz had rescued, saved his father in the camp, and he believed he'd ended up in England, and while he was here finishing his studies Alex was trying to trace this man.'

'And?'

'And he thought he was finally getting somewhere. People he talked to up here tried to sort of put him off, I mean his own prof warned him that there was a sort of moral vacuum in the camps where nothing was really normal, and he might find out things he didn't want to know, but Alex was determined, and he finally got track of someone in Bristol, and he went down to see him, and that was a few weeks back, and . . . well, he's sort of disappeared.'

'He didn't come back from Bristol?'

'Well, I think he did. I mean, he rang me, sounded excited, said he had a lead and was coming back that night. But I was going back home to my parents in Scotland for a few days and I don't know what happened. The others told me he never showed. And there's been no word since. And I've been worried . . . I mean, what's happened to him?'

She was a bonny lass, and she was close to tears.

Culpeper had leaned forward, patted the back of her hand. 'We'll see what we can do. Make some enquiries . . .'

'I don't know why we're bothering with this,' Farnsby moaned. 'I've just come out of a meeting with the Assistant Chief Constable, and it looks as though there's trouble brewing on our patch.'

'But you *have* made some enquiries about Isaacson,' Culpeper insisted.

Farnsby nodded unhappily. 'I've been across to the university, spoken to a few people. And interviewed some of the students at Alex Isaacson's digs. But it's difficult, sir, we don't even have any formal report on a missing person. I mean, Isaacson's a grown lad. Maybe he's just gone back home to Israel. We don't have the resources . . .'

'But what have you found out?' Culpeper persisted. Farnsby sighed, opened a file in front of him.

'I spoke to the students: they were expecting him back, he seems to have left his stuff at the house in Victoria Terrace, but he hasn't showed for a couple of weeks. None of them are close friends with him — just that girl, the only one interested really. From what I gathered, it's a case of unrequited passion.'

'She told me they were just friends.'

Farnsby shrugged. 'My guess is she would have liked something closer than that. Still . . . I then asked around in the department. They haven't seen him. His tutor — Professor Saul Davidson — was pretty forthcoming. Knew Isaacson pretty well, spoke highly of him as a student. Says he was going to get involved in that work at Abbey Head — the sea cave. But . . . knows nothing about his disappearance. But he did confirm one thing.'

'What's that?'

'He described it as an obsession. The thing Isaacson had about tracing some concentration camp guard called Otto Wenschoff. In Davidson's view the search would be doomed to disappointment. It was all pointless, he said: why dig up the past, that sort of thing.'

'Have you made any enquiries in Bristol?' Culpeper asked.

Farnsby snorted in exasperation. 'There's no way we can afford to make enquiries down there, sir! It seems Isaacson went to see some old codger in a nursing home — guy in his nineties, who knew something about it all but if Isaacson is supposed to have come back up here anyway—'

'So you haven't checked it out,' Culpeper asked, steel in his tone.

Farnsby hesitated, weighing up his courage. It lacked in the balance. 'I'll get on to it,' he said wearily.

Culpeper squirmed a little in satisfaction. Farnsby was the new kind of copper, the graduate who'd shot through to seniority without spending street time, and it was something Culpeper resented. Not enough to cause an active dislike — Farnsby wasn't really a bad copper, just too ambitious, and too inclined to pander to the brass. The Assistant Chief thought he was a golden boy. Culpeper enjoyed the golden boy spending time on boring, dogged paperwork and door-knocking. The Assistant Chief Constable . . . 'What sort of trouble were you saying the ACC was on about?' Culpeper asked diffidently.

'The Home Office and Special Branch have been tapping into the Internet — there's a whole lot of fuss going on, e-mails flying all over the place, all over these bloody illegal immigrants. Somebody on the south coast is trying to start a sort of action day.'

'So?'

'We've got our own group of illegals housed just north of here. And we've got our own group of roughnecks who'll be only too willing to join in a bit of mayhem. There's been a directive from the Home Office — try to keep the lid on things.'

'Ahhh.' Culpeper nodded thoughtfully. He cast his mind back to Macardle's leaving party at Ponteland: Sid Larson, hunched in the seminar room. Maybe that had been a dry run for the kind of trouble being expected. Or maybe just a fracas in a pub. They'd let Larson go, of course, with a warning, but Larson was never the kind to behave simply because he'd had a warning to stay out of trouble, He was attracted to it, like a rat to a rotting corpse. 'When is this action scheduled for?'

'Next week.' Farnsby eyed his senior officer carefully, a glint of hope in his eyes. 'I could concentrate on that, sir, if I didn't have to chase up these other matters. And with these illegals, we could be getting a lot of bad publicity as well as broken windows.'

Culpeper could almost hear the words of the Assistant Chief Constable. He grimaced, turned on his heel. 'I'll think about it,' he said and walked back to his room.

With a cup of coffee in front of him, Culpeper sat down behind his desk, half closed his eyes, and tried to concentrate. There were butterflies dancing in his head, fluttering memories he could not pin down, fleeting thoughts that came and went. Alex Isaacson . . . Sid Larson . . . Saul Davidson . . . illegal immigrants. They had all become jumbled in his mind.

But he was unlike Farnsby. He was old-fashioned, dogged, persistent — and ambition had long flown from his mind. He had had several disputes with Farnsby in the past over the way in which he kept old files, matters that had remained unresolved and probably never would see the light of day again. Farnsby was impatient, wanted decks to be cleared. Culpeper was different: a lifetime working on the Tyne and in Northumberland had given him experience, and memories . . . if only he could recapture them. Old files could do that.

Dusty files, stowed away in a storeroom.

He closed his eyes, and concentrated.

2

The breeze on the headland was stiff but the rainclouds had gone, and the afternoon sun was bright across the greensward. On the horizon a bank of cloud stretched, white and fluffy, while across the blue sky vapour trails faded slowly as the jet training flights that had screamed far above passed to distant thunder. Arnold stood on the headland, near the ruined walls of the ancient abbey, and wondered how it would have been here, all those years ago, when the abbey itself still flourished. Not very much different, he guessed: the headland grazed by scattered sheep, the stone walls enfolding other flocks, the manor house surrounded by farm buildings, and where he stood, probably a kitchen garden, or a midden, or an orchard. It was possible there had been outbuildings here, long since gone; maybe stone foundations of buildings belonging to the abbey lay buried at his feet. And maybe, over there where Hades Gate gaped to the sky, the monks would have chanted their exorcisms, overlaying the far more ancient incantations that shamans would have keened over the millennia.

He wondered what the monks would really have made of Hades Gate. They would have had a different name for it, no doubt, but for them he imagined it would always have had connotations of evil. He walked slowly across the short-cropped green of the headland, towards the fissure in the ground. He stood there looking down into it, staring at the gaping, bubbling rock, feeling a cold chill from the dark wound in the ground, and he wondered about the circumstances of that lonely railwayman's death. Maybe he had been drunk. Maybe it had been a wild night on the headland, as recent storms had shown. Maybe he had been at the end of his tether, feeling a strain that Arnold could not know about. The kind of strain that Chris Hayman seemed to be feeling.

It was clear to Arnold that Hayman was still finding it difficult to come to terms with life after his wife's death. There was an edginess about the man in the office: comments had been made about it among the other staff. He seemed distracted, daydreaming with a worried, haunted, almost despairing look on his face at times. Since the sea cave investigation had restarted, two days ago, he had been working on site, helping sift and clear rubble and detritus from the floor of the cave itself, trampled as it had been by policemen and forensic scientists. But somehow his heart did not seem to be in it: his actions were mechanical, listless. He spoke very little, simply followed instructions, but Arnold had the odd feeling that the man was watching him, as though in some odd manner he saw a form of salvation in his new friendship.

If that was what it could be called. The thought made Arnold uneasy. The relationship seemed to have become one best described as an emotional dependence, for Arnold did not care for Hayman particularly. He felt sorry for him, and wanted to help, but it was an unreal kind of friendship. And the manner in which Hayman seemed to hover at his shoulder, watching him distantly, disturbed Arnold. It was unnerving.

He heard a car horn, and turned. The Rover was coming towards him, along the newly laid track. Arnold raised a hand in greeting, and walked across to meet the car. It drew to a stop, and Professor Saul Davidson got out, tall, stooped, dressed casually in sweater, jeans and an old pair of trainers.

'So you managed to get away,' Arnold said.

'My first visit to the site,' Davidson replied, smiling, 'and having made so many promises to you, I had to make sure I turned up this time.'

Arnold shook his head. 'We've only just started to repair the ravages of the police inspection. I'm afraid much will have been destroyed by their trampling about in the sea cave. But I think there's still plenty for us to discover.'

Davidson looked about him, stooping slightly with the breeze at his back. He looked older than Arnold remembered. Possibly, it was the effect of the sunlight, glinting on his scalp, shining through his thinning grey hair. But there was still a whipcord strength in the man's leanness. He was staring towards the fissure in the ground. 'So that's what they call Hades Gate?'

Arnold nodded and led him across so that he could peer into its depths. Davidson was silent for a little while, contemplative. 'It reminds me a little of the *emotes*, although they were tied in with water veneration.'

'You've been to Mesoamerica?'

'I have. Quite an experience. The *cenotes* — they're really natural sinkholes in the limestone crust — were used in most instances as mundane sources of water but some were set aside as special. I visited the sacred *cenote* of Chichen Itza. Magnificently atmospheric. A major pilgrimage and sacrificial site for the ancient Maya. Votive offerings were thrown into its depths, dedicated to Kukulkan, the Feathered Serpent: artefacts, food, objects . . . and human beings. It was called the Well of Time.'

Arnold grunted. 'It has much in common with this, then. One of the local names for this fissure is the Well of Time. And if my theory is correct, and the artefacts we've found already in the sea cave were originally thrown down into this fissure, it matches Chichen Itza in other respects too.'

'The skeletal remains, you mean.' Davidson's voice was quiet. In a tone that was suddenly casual, he asked, 'Have the police reached any conclusions yet?'

'None that they've imparted to me.'

'And you think the man might have fallen into this fissure, lain there for years, and then . . .'

'Heavy rain, rock slide, I don't know. Maybe his remains only came down to the sea cave when we were there, in the rock fall Portia Tyrrel and I experienced. Who knows? Anyway, shall we go down now — so you can see things for yourself?'

They walked back to Davidson's Rover, and Arnold directed him along the track down to the beach and the small parking area that had been established at the edge of the newly constructed sea retaining wall. Davidson inspected the wall critically. 'Looks a bit hurried, bit flimsy to me,' he suggested. 'Do you think it'll withstand the storms that are bound to come next winter? It's pretty exposed here.'

Arnold shrugged. 'I've already made the point. Maybe it'll serve for now, but I think it will need deepening and widening, as you suggest, before we leave the site for the winter. It would be devastating if we were to lose the cave, now it's been opened.'

Most of the team had broken from their labours for a while to take coffee, at the makeshift hut near the cave entrance. Arnold introduced each member to Davidson. He shook hands, had a word with two of them whom he recognized as his own students. As they were talking Chris Hayman emerged from the sea cave. When he saw Arnold and Saul Davidson he hung back, seemingly reluctant to join the group. Arnold called him forward and was surprised at what seemed truculence on Hayman's part. Hayman shook hands, but kept his head averted as though in embarrassment, and barely spoke when Davidson asked him how the work was going. There was also a note of puzzlement in Davidson's voice. He glanced at Arnold, uncertainly, as though expecting some comment. Then the moment was gone, though as they walked towards the sea cave entrance Arnold caught Davidson glancing back, a slight frown on his lean features.

When they entered the cave, Arnold heard Davidson's intake of breath. His flashlight picked out the first sketchy intimations of carving, the first pigmentations on the wall depicting animals and flying humans, gleaming in the torchlight on the shiny rock face as they would have gleamed under rushlights for thousands of years. 'These would suggest shamanistic activity,' Davidson almost whispered. His awed tone skittered lightly, sibilant against the high roof, echoing as a faint susurration in the lobed chamber of the sea cave. He flashed his light along the roof. The beam wavered, then stopped. 'Look, you see those series of dots, or holes marked in the rock? No one knows what such markings mean now, but some eminent people argue they are the entoptic patterns that tribal societies saw in trances induced by plant hallucinogen . . .' The beam flickered further, pausing here and there on the ceiling of the cave. Excitement made Davidson's tone ragged, as though he had difficulty breathing. 'And here . . . is that the image of a footprint, carved in the rock?'

'It looks like it,' Arnold agreed. 'But the interpretation—'

'Ah, but don't you see? Evidence in Scandinavia suggests that such carvings have a logical meaning. The world of the dead is, naturally, underground. Consequently, this world is inverted in relation to the world we inhabit. So, it follows that the dead walk upside down, sometimes the soles of their feet touching ours. A shadowland. A track perhaps that allows the recently deceased to journey to the otherworld: dead men walking.'

They moved on. Arnold could almost feel the excited tension experienced by Saul Davidson. He exclaimed over the blue glow provided by the light from the blow-hole far above, and agreed with Arnold's suggested explanation. He inspected the rock fall that Arnold and Portia had experienced and shone the flashlight upwards. The police had cleared part of the site there, and removed much of the material that lay scattered about: animal and human bones, artefacts. Davidson shook his head sadly. 'Provenance will now be difficult to establish. But I think you might be right, about the fissure on the headland — Hades Gate. It would account for the noises you described as being heard up above, and as far as I can see, though there is no daylight to be discerned down here, like you I think there is a kind of chimney here, a wide crack in the rock, leading upwards, twisting . . .'

They were there for more than two hours. The work team came in and carried on behind them, while Davidson examined every inch of the wall, exclaiming over the petroglyphs, marvelling at the mysterious carvings, discussing ideas and theories with Arnold. When they finally emerged from the cave, narrowing their eyes against the brightness of the sky, dusting themselves down, Davidson was wearing a wide smile. 'It's beyond what I had been expecting. There's years of work there, I appreciate that now. It's a marvellous find, Landon, and I'm really looking forward to joining you here — and I'm grateful for the invitation you've extended. It's a shame that so much damage has been caused by the police—'

'Clodhoppers all, hey?' a voice called out to them. Arnold turned. Leaning against the wall of the makeshift hut was the bulky, middle-aged form of Detective Chief Inspector Culpeper.

The policeman smiled expansively and walked ponderously towards them. 'So, how are things going?'

Arnold hesitated. 'Well enough. Are you here . . . on official business?'

Culpeper laughed, a great rumbling in his deep chest. 'No, I've got an appointment in about fifteen minutes up at the manor house. Time to spare, so I thought I'd come down, have another look around, see whether we've really messed up your work.'

'It's been made more difficult,' Arnold admitted stiffly.

He never felt relaxed in Culpeper's presence.

'Aye,' Culpeper reflected. 'Skeletons can do that.' He sniffed at the wind. 'Sea breeze. North coast. Can't beat it, you know. Grand day like this, up at Seahouses . . . instead of which . . .' He squinted at Arnold's companion. 'So, you going to introduce us?'

Hurriedly, Arnold apologized. 'I'm sorry, Inspector—'

'*Detective Chief* Inspector,' Culpeper admonished him.

In confusion, Arnold turned to his companion. 'This is Saul Davidson.'

Culpeper shook his great head slowly, almost sadly, at Arnold's lack of protocol. '*Professor* Saul Davidson.' Davidson smiled, glanced at Arnold with the hint of one lowered eyelid. 'It's of no consequence. I'll settle for mere Mr.'

'So do surgeons,' Culpeper grunted. He eyed Davidson carefully. 'I've heard of you, Professor. How long you been working at the university?'

'For more years than I care to remember,' Davidson replied easily.

'Have we met before?'

'I think I would have remembered.'

Culpeper probably detected the slight hint of irony in the remark, as Arnold did. He glowered a little. 'I have a feeling . . . our paths haven't crossed?'

'Not to my knowledge,' Davidson replied soberly. 'I've tended to stay out of trouble, on the whole.'

'Hmm.' Culpeper shook his head in vague indecision. 'I just get this feeling . . . Still, old men like me, they get fuddled, you know? Forget things. One thing I haven't forgot though, is I need to have a word with you.'

'Yes?' Davidson asked, raising his eyebrows interrogatively.

'Not now.' Culpeper waved a hand. 'Not here. I think I should come along to your office at the university. Have a chat.'

'Any time, Chief Inspector,' Davidson replied, in a slightly amused tone. 'I'll get out the sherry.'

Culpeper didn't enjoy being patronized. He patted his gut with a stubborn pride. 'I'm a beer man, Professor Davidson. But don't bother getting any in. I'll arrange an appointment for tomorrow, or the next day?'

'To discuss what?'

Culpeper inspected the sky, watching the wheeling birds. 'Gulls, fulmars, you get all sorts along these cliffs. At one time, sea eagles, I guess. But not now.' His glance slipped back to Davidson. 'About what? Just one of your students, what else?'

'Whose name is?'

Culpeper's eyes were challenging suddenly. 'Isaacson. You know him well, apparently. And as you know, he's gone missing.'

'I've already spoken to—'

'In a day or so,' Culpeper interrupted cheerily. 'I'll be in touch.'

He nodded to Arnold, turned and walked slowly away, with a ponderous gait. He had clearly left his car at the headland, Arnold realized. He could find it heavy going, walking up the steep beach road. But he was disinclined to offer him a lift.

'You know him well?' Davidson asked, in a slightly distant tone.

'Our paths have crossed from time to time,' Arnold replied dismissively.

Davidson was silent for a little while. 'Anyway,' he said at last, eyeing the labouring bulk of the policeman struggling across the beach, 'I'll take my leave of you. I'd better offer the Detective Chief Inspector a lift up the hill. As for the work here, and my involvement, I'll let you have a schedule of my availability, send it to you in a day or so once I've sorted out my university commitments. And there's a new group of students I can brief to work with you down here. Looking at that rather flimsy sea wall, I think the project should press on.'

The others were coming out of the sea cave, feet crunching on pebbles and sand, their work over for the afternoon. Davidson glanced at them, was about to move off when he hesitated, looked back again, and then suddenly turned and left Arnold, walked back towards the group emerging from the cave. He stopped in front of Chris Hayman, spoke to him for a moment, and then extended his hand. Reluctantly, it seemed to Arnold, Hayman extended his own. Then he turned away, to gather up his rucksack near the hut. Davidson came up to Arnold, nodding. 'Thought so. There was something about him. I never really forget a face.'

'I don't follow.'

Professor Saul Davidson jerked his head back towards the man with whom he had just shaken hands. 'Chris Hayman. The name didn't ring a bell at first — God, it must be twenty-five years or more . . . but I thought I knew him.' He began to walk away towards his car. 'I'm surprised he didn't recognize me before I did him. Students tend to remember teachers rather than the other way around.' He caught the surprise in Arnold's eyes. 'That's right. Chris Hayman used to be one of my students . . . a long time ago.'

3

Culpeper always felt uneasy in grand houses. He was an old-fashioned copper, one who'd been brought up as a child in a terrace house on the outskirts of Chester le Street, and who had been proud to put on the uniform that gave him responsibility for dealing with tearaways in Shields, along the banks of the Tyne, and eventually working in the pit villages of Northumberland. The odd fracas at the harbour in Amble, a pub brawl in Ashington, a bit of breaking and entering at Warkworth, these were all matters he took in his stride. They were his people and he could understand them, talk to them, bully them if needs be. But stepping into big country houses was another thing.

He'd had to do it from time to time, of course: hunt saboteurs sometimes made it necessary for him to get involved with the hunting fraternity. There had been stately home robberies by gangs coming in from Wearside, Manchester and Liverpool; and there were many occasions when he had been called upon as a young copper to patrol grounds when some politician or other flew in from London to take part in discussions with wealthy supporters. They weren't bad times either: a bottle of whisky was often slipped out to warm the lads on duty.

But he'd never got over the feeling of being in the wrong place, when he entered a country mansion.

Abbey Manor certainly was that. Culpeper didn't know too much about such places, but he could appreciate grandeur when he saw it. And it made him feel smaller, in some way he was unable to define. When a visit to Abbey Manor had been called for, he had even considered sending Farnsby to deal with the matter.

Farnsby had come into his office with a file in his hand. 'I've now managed to get the information you were calling for, from Bristol.'

'Yes?'

Farnsby had bridled a little at the dismissiveness in Culpeper's tone. 'You said it had to be given priority, sir.'

'So tell me.'

'Alex Isaacson. It seems he went to Bristol to talk to an old man who used to live up here at one time — went down to Bristol in the eighties, to die. He's still alive, just. In a nursing home. In his nineties now, failing a bit physically as you'd imagine, but still pretty sharp.'

'What's his connection with Isaacson?' Culpeper asked vaguely.

Farnsby was patient. 'No connection with Isaacson, as such. You'll recall sir,' he went on with heavy emphasis, 'that Isaacson seems to have been intent on tracing someone called Otto Wenschoff. So Professor Davidson told me at the university.'

'Ah, yes,' Culpeper said, wrinkling his nose. 'Saul Davidson . . . I wish I could remember . . .'

Farnsby paused, portentously. 'Do you want me to go on, sir?'

Culpeper's already piggy eyes narrowed further at the veiled insolence in Farnsby's tone. 'Otto Wenschoff,' he rumbled.

'That's right. Apparently, a guard at Auschwitz.'

'And this man in Bristol?'

'Gave Isaacson a lead.' Farnsby leaned forward and placed the folder gently upon the desk in front of Culpeper. I've made all the relevant notes in there.'

'I'd rather you told me about it.'

Farnsby straightened. He smiled thinly, as though he had expected the comment and oddly enough he seemed satisfied with the request. 'Interesting story, actually. The man in Bristol — name of Jack Svensson — he worked in the pits for years, up at Ashington, but became friendly with a man he'd first met in lodgings. They probably became friendly because they were both outsiders, having some difficulty with the English language, refugees from Europe at the end of the war. Svensson was from Norway. Anyway, they stayed in touch for a number of years, drank together regularly, until the seventies.'

Culpeper felt the first stir of reluctant interest. He observed Farnsby sourly. 'You're going to tell me this other man was Otto Wenschoff?'

There was an edge of triumph in Farnsby's smile. 'I'm not saying that, sir. The man Svensson became friendly with, he called himself Arthur Winder. He and Svensson lost touch with each other. Svensson doesn't know what became of him — though there is a note in the file . . . CID in Bristol felt the old man was being a bit evasive at this point. Anyway, old man Svensson did give Alex Isaacson a pointer. He advised him to go talk to Hall Gabriel.'

'And just who the hell is Hall Gabriel?' Culpeper snarled.

'He's the owner of Abbey Manor. He was brought up on Tyneside, was around here at the relevant time. Went away, made a mint of money, came back north to his roots.'

'And Isaacson was advised to go see him?'

'That's right. And we have the evidence of a phone call to say Isaacson was returning north. But he never showed at his digs. And he's disappeared, according to your young lady. So, the question is, did he go to Abbey Manor and then . . . disappear?'

'It's all in the file?'

'Yes, sir.'

'Then you follow it up.'

Farnsby retrieved the file and turned to leave. There was something about his eagerness that made Culpeper suspicious. 'There's something else?'

Farnsby's back stiffened. Reluctantly, he turned. 'Well . . . there is something else, but not related to this . . .'

'Then what?'

Farnsby hesitated. 'The other thing . . . that identity disc that was discovered in the sea cave.'

'What about it?'

'The LNER records, they've now been checked, and the number stamped on the disc, well, we can put a name to the railwayman.'

'And?'

'The railwayman's name was Arthur Winder.'

Culpeper sat glaring at Farnsby. He began to drum his fingers on the table in slow irritation. Farnsby would have walked out of the room on this one, tying two things together, keeping the matter to himself, showing Culpeper up in his last weeks in office. He'd have gone to the ACC, perhaps pointing out what his own perspicacity had achieved, while Culpeper blundered about, lolling behind his desk like an old, land-trapped walrus.

Culpeper extended his hand. 'Leave the file with me.'

Now, in the hallway at Abbey Manor, Culpeper began to feel impatient. He had the feeling there were some interesting questions to be asked, some ends to be tied together — but he was being kept waiting. And there was still something else that was niggling at him. He had decided that when he got back to Morpeth he was going to have to do a serious trawl through the old records. There was some gleam in the gathering gloom of his mind, a pinpoint of light that was attracting him. A memory needed dredging up, there was something in all this that disturbed him. An old man's memory . . .

'Mr Culpeper?' Sean Corman's tone was polite, but Culpeper knew all about restrained insolence. He'd heard it in the voices of a thousand villains over the years, and he had the strong suspicion that Corman would not have been too far distant from a bit of thuggery in his time. But wealthy men often kept leashed dogs like this one, for their own protection — or image.

'Mr Gabriel will see you in the library.'

He led the way.

Hall Gabriel was at ease. He was dressed in a casual shirt, light blue sweater, immaculately cut slacks and golf shoes. He was seated at a polished mahogany table, just in front of the window: his face was slightly flushed, and there was a tumbler of whisky beside his left elbow. It was clear he had just returned from exercise on a nearby golf course, and had already taken a few drinks before the one he had presently half consumed. He lifted a hand in casual greeting, but did not bother to rise. 'Detective Chief Inspector Culpeper, I believe. Sean, get the man a drink.'

Culpeper did not care for *the man*, but was disinclined to forgo a good whisky. 'Make it a small one, if you don't mind.'

'So none of this nonsense about drinking on duty, hey?'

Hall Gabriel laughed, and supped his own whisky. 'I guess you've been around long enough not to care.'

'Something like that, Mr Gabriel.' Culpeper stood at the library window looking out over the headland, the abbey ruins, and the distant blue line of the sea. 'Quite a view.'

'I've always thought so,' Gabriel agreed. 'Ever since I was a kid.'

'Yes, I understand you were a local lad.' Culpeper accepted the cut glass from Corman. He met the man's glance: Corman's eyes were cold, with ill-concealed hostility.

'Local lad made good,' Gabriel corrected. 'As you probably know. Used to admire this place as a kid, and, in the end, things went so well I was able to come back and achieve a dream.'

'But you won't spend a great deal of time here, of course.'

'Business will always call, naturally. Though, I hope, much of it can now be transacted at a distance — new technologies and all that.' Gabriel smiled thinly. 'Even so, it's always a good thing to show yourself to the workers from time to time — kicking arses is always necessary if a business is to prosper.'

Culpeper sipped his whisky: it was an expensive malt.

He would have expected no less. 'You spent much time in the north-east over recent years, Mr Gabriel?'

'Not a great deal. I've travelled the world.'

'But twenty years ago?'

'I was around. Here and about. And now I'm back, to relax, enjoy myself a bit more.'

'Your relaxation must have been disturbed when Alex Isaacson called.'

Hall Gabriel glanced briefly towards Sean Corman, standing with hands clasped in front of him, silent, to one side of Culpeper. 'Who?'

Culpeper made no reply for a moment: he sipped his whisky thoughtfully. 'Did you ever come across Arthur Winder, in the old days?'

'I don't believe I've ever heard the name before,' Gabriel replied, but his mouth had stiffened, and his tone was guarded.

'What about Otto Wenschoff?'

'Sounds foreign.'

Culpeper nodded. 'Yes. Mr Wenschoff, it seems, was a guard in the concentration camp at Auschwitz, during the war.'

'Never was there,' Gabriel said with a grin. 'Wasn't me, guv.'

'So why would Alex Isaacson come to see you about him?'

'I haven't the faintest idea.'

There was a short silence. Culpeper sighed, shook his head doubtfully. 'But he did come here?'

Gabriel finished his drink, gestured to Corman. The big man came forward silently, took the glass, replenished it and placed it in front of his employer. Then he took up station again, just behind Culpeper. 'What is this all about?' Gabriel asked quietly.

Culpeper shrugged. 'It seems Alex Isaacson, a student at Newcastle University, has gone missing. Now, we know he was pursuing some individual quest of his own, apart from his academic studies. He was trying to trace this man Otto Wenschoff. He finally managed to make contact with an ex-miner from Ashington — Jack Svensson — who is now living in Bristol. Dying, it seems. He's had a long innings. Isaacson went to see him, and was advised to come back north and see you, if he wanted further information about Otto Wenschoff. Now why would he do that, Mr Gabriel?'

'I can only repeat: I haven't the faintest idea. I've never even heard of Otto Wenschoff, before you mentioned the name.'

'And you haven't heard of Arthur Winder, either?'

'Like I said, I've no recollection.' Gabriel waited a little while, and then said, 'I've been playing golf, Mr Culpeper. I hope this isn't going to take too long. When I've finished this drink, I'd like to take a shower—'

'This Otto Wenschoff,' Culpeper persisted. 'We have reason to believe that he and Arthur Winder were possibly one and the same person.'

Gabriel puffed out his lean cheeks in exasperation. 'So?'

'So it was Arthur Winder's skeleton — we think — that was found in the sea cave, at the foot of the cliff over there.'

There was a long silence. Gabriel raised his glass, stared at its amber contents. 'You think,' he said slowly.

'We're following lines of enquiry, which make us believe—'

'You *think*. Look here, Culpeper, I'm tired of this. You come here and ask me about two people I've never met, whose names I've never heard of, and you ask me to explain why a complete stranger — this Isaacson fellow should come making enquiries of me here. I've already told you — I don't know Isaacson, don't know why he came here, don't know

Wenschoff or this Winder person . . . and as far as I've heard, if those bones in the sea cave are what remains of Winder, they're old bones. That means he will have died years ago. Long before I ever came to Abbey Manor!'

He finished his drink with one long gulp, and hoisted himself to his feet. Anger was suddenly spilling from him as he crooked a finger at Culpeper. 'I'm tired of this hassle. Come with me, Detective Chief Inspector! While you're around nannying after some young whippersnapper of a student, and chasing up twenty-year-old ghosts, other things are happening! Follow me.'

He marched out of the library and into the hall.

Culpeper, unwilling to waste the whisky, downed his drink quickly and followed. He was aware of Sean Corman, soft-footed, just behind his shoulder.

Gabriel strode out through the front entrance of the house, down the steps and turned right to what would have been the stable area at one time. Behind the walled garden the old stables had been converted into garages. Gabriel looked back towards Corman and jerked his head. The man came walking past Culpeper quickly, and headed for the garages. He already had the doors open when Culpeper and Gabriel arrived.

Inside there were two cars: a Jaguar and a Porsche. The windscreens of both vehicles had been smashed, and deep score marks ran along the highly polished length of each car.

'Now then,' Gabriel said, breathless with anger. 'Let's get some things in perspective. You come out here, asking me about things I know nothing about. Long dead men, dying men, students with bees in their bonnets. I'm a reasonable man, and a wealthy one, so damage of this kind isn't going to edge me towards bankruptcy, but try to see it from my point of view! You ask me damned foolish questions, at the same time this kind of thing's going on!'

'What exactly happened here?' Culpeper asked.

'A couple of nights ago,' Sean Corman advised quietly. 'The garages were broken into. Nothing was stolen. This is just vandalism.'

'Any ideas about who might have done it?'

Corman glanced at Gabriel, and shook his head. His voice was cold. 'Not at the moment.'

'No particular enemies you can think of?' Culpeper asked.

'All businessmen have enemies. But a particular one . . . not at the moment,' Gabriel repeated viciously. 'And let's get one thing clear, Culpeper. I don't give a damn about your Isaacson — yes, he came here, like you, asking stupid questions that I couldn't answer and he got shown the door, rapidly. I don't give a damn about him, whether he's disappeared or not. I don't give a damn about this Winder character, or whether he had another name or not. But I do give a damn when my property is damaged, my privacy invaded. But don't get me wrong.'

He gestured towards Corman, to close the garage doors. 'I've no intention of seeking your help, Culpeper, or any other plod in the north. I have my own ways of dealing with problems, and they don't involve running squealing like a stuck pig to the police. But I'll tell you this, when I find out just who's been seen prowling around Abbey Manor, when I find out who's broken in here and done this, believe me, I'll know just how to deal with the situation. And it won't involve you bloody coppers!'

'Mr Gabriel, I would advise—'

'I don't want your advice, any more than I want your questions or your assistance,' Gabriel snapped angrily. 'I just want you off my property!'

* * *

Culpeper was still seething hours later, back at his office in Ponteland. He marched to Farnsby's office to be told he was out. Culpeper snarled that he wanted to see the inspector immediately on his return. In an attempt to bring some order into his mind Culpeper strode down to the archive room, and began to hunt through the old files that had been stored here for years, and prior to that in the archive in Morpeth.

Something was digging at his memory. He was unable to pin it down, but he knew there was the chance the answer he sought was in the old files, somewhere . . . Dust rose dancing in the air as he pulled down old folders, hunted through sloppily maintained indexes, dredged back through the years of his career along the Tyne, in Newcastle, in Shields, in the pit villages of Northumberland. Irritated, he banged about to no avail, until eventually he went back upstairs to the canteen, got himself some coffee and a ham sandwich, and munched moodily, avoided by other colleagues present. They knew better than to approach him when he was clearly in such a bad temper.

Snatches of conversation drifted across to him as he sat there. '. . . chance for overtime, at least. According to the briefing, it'll be riot shield stuff . . .' There was some laughter, a bit of ribaldry that was lost to him as he chewed doggedly away, trying to marshal his thoughts, dragoon his memories into order.

'It'll be just like old times,' he heard someone say. He glanced across to the other table: Percy Thomas, never made it out of uniform, but a solid enough copper. Sergeant, now, and like Culpeper, near to retirement. 'At least I won't be in the front line, not like last time.'

Culpeper turned his head, staring at the sergeant. Percy Thomas caught the glance, raised his eyebrows.

'What time you talking about, Percy?'

'Miners' strike. Never really approved of all that, any more than you did, I recall. I mean, those poor bloody miners, led by rabble-rousers, they were always going to be on a loser. And so were we. Aye, we got our overtime and all that, but I didn't like bein' spat on by miners' wives, and have all that criticism in the press. We was just doing our job, man, but you'd think we were the bloody Gestapo!'

It churned in Culpeper's mind. Not the Gestapo . . .

He finished his sandwich, drained his coffee cup and made his way back down to the archive room. There was a clearer point of reference now, an old, half-ignored, half-forgotten report. Names, places . . . identifications. That was the difference between him and bloody Farnsby, he exulted, as he finally drew out a dog-eared file. Experience, doggedness, the refusal to accept defeat.

He was back at his desk, calmer, the warmth of a satisfied triumph in his veins, when Farnsby finally returned to the office. He tapped on the door. 'I'm told you wanted to see me, sir? I was down in Newcastle today — we've had the reports of likely disturbances over these immigrants, and the likely hot spots have been identified. It looks like we're going to be involved in the county. There'll be a demonstration in Grey Street, though they think they've got everything sorted, to contain it. But I'll have to see the Assistant Chief Constable — he's asked me to co-ordinate the response we're—'

'Stuff that,' Culpeper interrupted pleasantly. 'Talk to me about that guy in Bristol. Svensson. Bristol CID interviewed him?'

'That's right. We gave them the necessary information—'

'Couldn't be bothered to go down there yourself?' Farnsby coloured slightly. 'We've got more important things to deal with, sir. There's not even been any formal missing persons report over Isaacson yet. Nobody's really interested—'

'I'm interested.'

'Yes, sir, but priorities.'

Culpeper told him obscenely what he could do with his priorities. With a grim satisfaction, he growled, 'The information you got from Bristol. How did you get it?'

Farnsby hesitated. 'Phone call.'

'And you took notes.'

'Yes, sir.'

'Those are the notes in the file. The one you gave me.' Farnsby nodded, tight-lipped. He stood very straight.

'What's the problem, sir?'

Culpeper scowled at him, his eyes mean and narrowed. 'This Svensson character . . . what was he reported as having said, in advising Isaacson?'

Farnsby frowned. 'He told him to go to see Mr Gabriel.'

'Precisely that? Think back, Inspector Farnsby.'

Farnsby was flustered. 'I took notes, I wrote it down . . .'

'Who was Isaacson advised to go to see?'

There was a tense, strained silence. Farnsby stood rigid, thinking. His face was pale, and he was containing his anger at being cross-questioned in this manner, but his anger was also stained with concern. 'I don't know that—'

'Was there a name really mentioned?' Culpeper demanded. 'There wasn't, was there? My guess is, Svensson told Bristol CID that he advised Isaacson to go see the owner of Abbey Manor. That was what you were told. And, smart-arse that you are, you checked who the owner of the manor is. Hall Gabriel.'

Farnsby licked his lips. 'I've got other things on . . . I thought it would help . . .'

'When Svensson lived up north the property wasn't owned by Hall Gabriel, so he wasn't meaning Gabriel. He meant the previous owner.' Culpeper sneered. He leaned back in his chair, content. 'Farnsby, you're a *prat*!'

CHAPTER FOUR

1

The publicity surrounding the opening of the sea cave meant that for a few days afterwards there was a steady stream of visitors to the site. In marshalling them, and obtaining maximum benefit for the department — and herself — Karen Stannard was indefatigable. She brought them down to the beach regularly, politicians and patrons, publicists and palaeontologists, and she sparkled about the site, explaining the storms that had washed out the cave opening, discussing the meaning of the finds discovered within the lobed chamber, giving impromptu lectures on the people who would have used and inhabited and worshipped at the ritual site here, and elsewhere along the ancient coast. She glittered, she was in her element, and Arnold could only stand back and marvel.

Less welcome, but equally inevitable were the sensation-seekers who had been drawn by the story of the bones in the cave, pestering the team to try to gain access to gape and seek souvenirs. There were also the alternative religion enthusiasts seeking the meaning of life and death, relationships with the cosmos, the influence of the stars and the convergence of imagined ley lines. They clustered occasionally on the headland, and on the beach, chanting mantras and making strange humming sounds. By and large, Arnold was left to deal with those. When the important people came with Karen he was expected merely to stand by looking wise while she expounded — being thrown the occasional question to field, like a performing dog leaping to snatch a bone thrown by his mistress.

He found it enervating, the publicity visits from Karen, so when he emerged, tired and thirsty from the sea cave to refresh himself with a coffee, just an hour after she had left with one of her gaping contingents, he was slightly irritated to see Daniel Gibbs walking across the stony beach towards him. Gibbs was dressed informally, but smartly in casual jacket and slacks, and with his hair blowing in the wind he looked younger, somehow.

'Ah, Mr Landon,' Gibbs called out, advancing towards him. 'How are things going?'

'She's gone,' Arnold said, more abruptly than he meant.

Gibbs slowed, coloured slightly, and then stopped by the sea wall, glancing about him. 'Who?'

'Karen.' Arnold hesitated, suddenly feeling ashamed at his brusqueness. 'You like a coffee?'

'That would be civil of you, yes.' Gibbs followed him as he walked towards the hut. 'I heard there was a group coming along to the site this afternoon. I thought I'd stop by — I was in the neighbourhood. Returning to the old estates and all that.' He flickered a sheepish glance at Arnold. 'And I suppose I was . . . hoping to have a word with Karen.'

Arnold had seen it before. She could be like a flame to these moths of men: they saw in her something exciting and desirable and beautiful, and were drawn by her glow. But they didn't have to work with her. Arnold knew she could eat them for breakfast, the deadly female of the species. That didn't mean she wasn't exciting and desirable and beautiful within the office, he conceded to himself as he stirred milk into the coffee mugs. It was just that he could get annoyed by the simplicity of some of her admirers, who saw only the public, shimmering displays she could produce.

He brought the mugs out of the hut. Daniel Gibbs was standing a little way off, staring out to sea. A purple bruising of cloud edged the horizon. 'Not more storms, I hope,' he said as Arnold offered him the steaming mug.

'Storms are the last thing we want, while we're working at the cave.'

They sat down side by side on the concrete blocks of the sea wall that had recently been constructed. Gibbs sipped at the hot coffee. 'Karen . . . I hear she's doing an impressive job down here, with the visitors, I mean.' He hesitated, glancing uncertainly at Arnold. 'I get the impression . . . I mean . . . Is there any reason why she's still unattached?'

There had been vague gossip about lesbian tendencies around the office ever since Karen Stannard had arrived, rumours that she had even tended to encourage at one time for reasons best known to herself. But Arnold gave them little credence. And it was none of his business anyway. 'I think it's just she's a career woman,' he replied shortly.

'Or maybe not yet found the right man,' Gibbs murmured, brightening somewhat at the thought.

'Could be.'

They were silent for a little while. Behind them, in the sea cave, the rest of the team continued their work. There were only two there today, apart from Arnold; both students, keen, a little clumsy in their approach, but well-meaning in their enthusiasm.

'I used to come down here quite a bit, when I was a kid,' Gibbs announced meditatively. 'Sea pools over there, fishing for crab. And fossil hunting — stuff washed out of the cliff. Never very successful. Always a bit lonely.'

'No local children to spend time with?' Arnold asked, curious.

Gibbs shook his head, brushing the hair back from his eyes. 'No, not really. You see, I didn't spend all that much time here at the manor. When my father moved into residence to take up his inheritance after grandfather died, he had just left the army but there was still enough money to buy the things he thought were important. Like a public school education for me. But the result was I was away from Abbey Manor most of the time, at boarding school in the Midlands. The result was I never got to know any of the children at the local schools around here. Not that there were very many kids. We were pretty isolated here. There was just Abbey village.'

Arnold winced. He knew all about Abbey village.

'And I wasn't encouraged to get to know those people who worked on the farms for us,' Gibbs continued. 'As the various holdings got sold off, strangers moved in anyway.'

'But you still saw Abbey Manor as home.'

'Oh, yes, indeed.' Gibbs looked around him, glanced up at the sweep of the headland, the ruined abbey and the beetling cliff behind them. 'I loved it here, even though, as I said, I felt a bit . . . isolated. By the time I was in my teens, there was just me and my father. And he wasn't a warm man. His experiences during the war had made him somewhat introverted, irascible at times. He could be difficult to live with, particularly after my mother died. In fact, even when I was here I somehow contrived to stay out of his way as much as possible. It's not that he was violent or anything — though he insisted on rather high standards of behaviour. He could be a bit of a martinet. Army training, I suppose. To be honest, school was a relief, and if I could wangle an invitation to visit other chaps during the holidays, I did so, to avoid coming back to stay with the old man. Even so, I did love it here. The headland, the beach . . .'

'You must regret losing Abbey Manor,' Arnold suggested, aware of a certain melancholy in Gibbs's tone.

'Of course I do,' Gibbs replied, nodding, 'but there's always been a certain inevitability to it. I mean, the economics of it just didn't make sense — and I'm no estate manager. I managed to struggle on after my father died, about ten years ago, but I was never really going to make a go of it.' He was silent for a little while, frowning. He looked uncertainly at Arnold. 'He killed himself, you know. Shot himself in the head.'

There was a sudden, awkward silence. Arnold glanced at Gibbs, trying to find the right words. 'I'm sorry . . . I wasn't aware . . .'

Gibbs shrugged wearily. 'Ha, it's all old news really. I've ceased wondering about it. I was at Cambridge then, doing research. Chemistry. We got a phone call. My mother had been dead about four years then. I thought at the time maybe he couldn't face life without her any longer . . .'

Arnold thought briefly about Chris Hayman, uncertain, trying to draw his new existence around him like a ragged cloak.

'But the more I thought about it, I realized I was just romanticizing,' Gibbs went on. 'It wasn't like they were close, or that it was a great love. I mean, it just wasn't that kind of marriage, you know what I mean? She was the young-est daughter of a wealthy family in Ayrshire — he met her through a brother officer in the army. I think now that he married her, as men often did in like circumstances, in the expectation that she'd bring money to the marriage. For the continuation of the family jewel, Abbey Manor. It didn't work out that way. There was some money . . . but it wasn't significant.' He hesitated, frowning thoughtfully. 'Don't get me wrong, I don't think that affected their marriage — really, there was no great friction between them. They just tended to . . . ignore each other, go their own ways, I suppose. I don't even recall him being greatly grief-stricken when cancer took her.'

'Do you know now, why he took his own life?' Arnold asked in spite of himself, curious even though he felt he was intruding.

Gibbs sipped at his coffee, stared out to sea. 'I can't be sure, but I suspect it was something to do with his career in the army. He left the army under a cloud, you see, and it was like a canker growing in him over the years, ever since the end of the war. A sense of injustice, maybe. Or it could have been something else, I don't know.' He leaned forward, picked up a pebble and inspected it, before throwing it into the sea. He seemed uncertain whether to go on. 'You see, my father — Major Gibbs, he always insisted everyone called him Major — he was a man of strong views. Saw himself as a man of action, but he could fly into uncontrollable rages, so sometimes the action was rather . . . over the top, you know? He had a wide and eclectic range of dislikes: he hated the Labour Party, cats, the destitute of Tyneside, low-flying aircraft, foxes, Mormons, sycamore trees, the Germans, in fact, anyone from across the Channel. Not necessarily in that order. But as to why he shot himself, who knows? His reactions to the most mundane things or situations could be violent. Perhaps it was something he read in the paper that morning. Something that made him feel life was no longer worth living.' He was silent for a while. 'Or maybe it was self-loathing.'

The silence grew around them, broken only by the surging crash of the sea on the rocks, and the wild, keening cry of wheeling gulls, circling in the thermals high above Abbey Head.

'Did your father leave no . . . message?'

'Nothing,' Gibbs replied. 'And I was living my own life, I suppose I felt irritated having to give it up, return here, try to make a go of the estate. So I didn't pay too much attention to a lot of the paraphernalia he'd left behind in his study, the detritus of death. There was a stack of stuff in his study at the manor. I went through his papers, of course, and I must say I was pretty appalled by some of the stuff I came across.'

'How do you mean?'

'Oh, you know, right-wing rubbish,' Gibbs said uneasily. 'Pamphlets. Books. Britain for the British. The kind of inflammatory stuff that gets chanted by the National Front yobbos. I didn't understand it. I mean, he'd seen some nasty stuff during the war, believe me. It's why he had such a dislike for the Germans. Not just the Nazis, I tell you, he saw East Europeans in the same light. But the Nazis had been right wing, fascists. When I read this stuff it seemed to me he'd become almost like them, emotionally.' He grunted in dissatisfaction. 'No, that's not quite right. I threw the stuff out, anyway. Pornography. Burned most of it, in fact. And I can't really believe that it had an influence upon his decision to kill himself.' He glanced at Arnold, puzzlement in his tone. 'Awful decision to make, don't you think? To kill yourself?'

Arnold made no reply, thinking again of Hayman's wife.

He wondered whether Hayman agonized over the reasons for her depression. They sat silently for a while until at last Gibbs drained his mug, handed it back to Arnold. 'Been going on a bit, haven't I?'

'That's all right,' Arnold replied a little uncomfortably.

'But the answer to the original question is yes, I miss owning Abbey Manor. And I suppose I could have wished . . .' Gibbs hesitated, glancing again at Arnold. 'I don't think my father would have entirely approved.'

'Of what?'

'Of my selling the property to Hall Gabriel.' Gibbs wrinkled his nose thoughtfully. 'A local man, of course, but I've no recollection of him, from my childhood. He's older than I, and though he says he remembers seeing me as a child about the manor — he used to go poaching in the woods, he tells me — I certainly don't remember him. But my father would probably not have approved of the sale to Mr Gabriel. He would have had views about the man's origins, and maybe how he made his money.'

'He's just a businessman, I understand.'

'Ah, yes . . .' Gibbs sniffed and looked about him. 'It's just that at one time there were rumours, it seems. I don't know a great deal about it, but there's been some local gossip, I understand, about how he got started. He was in business with a man called Angell. Gabriel and Angell, quite a name for a haulage firm, don't you think?' He laughed briefly, shook his head. 'But something went wrong with it all, and Hall Gabriel was the one who came out ahead. I heard somewhere that his erstwhile partner Angell ended up embittered, on the dust heap. I don't really know. Anyway,

Gabriel moved away. His business grew quickly. Got lucky. I don't know. He did boast to me about it, but I'm not that interested, really. Except in the money, when it was offered. But I don't think Major Henry Gibbs would have approved. He was quite a snob.'

He looked at Arnold, shrugged and gave a lopsided smile. 'Maybe he brought his son up to be the same.'

* * *

At the university, there seemed to be few people wandering about. Half-term, Culpeper concluded, as he made his way to Professor Saul Davidson's rooms. He climbed the narrow stairs, tapped on the door, and waited. After a short interval he heard a brief scuffling, and the door opened. Davidson stood there, in his shirt-sleeves, slightly stooped, his dark, greying hair untidy, a little harassed. 'Sorry about that. Just getting some books and papers out of the way. Please come in, Mr Culpeper.'

'We did have an appointment.'

Davidson nodded vigorously. 'Of course. But you know how things are, catching up with marking and that. Would you like some coffee?'

Culpeper eyed the machine perched on the bookshelf and decided to pass on the offer. 'No, I'm okay, really. Cosy little set-up you have here.'

'Cluttered, you mean. But, home from home,' Davidson grinned almost sheepishly. He brushed back an errant lock of hair from his eyes, as he checked the coffee machine.

'Where is home?' Culpeper asked in an innocent tone.

'Jesmond.'

'But you're not local, of course.'

'I almost feel like it,' Davidson replied, as he poured himself some coffee into a stained mug. 'Do take a seat — that battered one over there . . . I was born in the United States, spent a certain amount of time in Switzerland, visited Israel for a while, but I've been here so long that I think I'm *almost* accepted now.'

'You've not got the Geordie accent, man,' Culpeper smiled, spreading himself into the stuffed comfort of an ancient armchair that had seen much better days. 'Without it, you'll always be an outsider.'

'That may be so,' Davidson agreed, 'but I've never really been made to feel that. An outsider, I mean.'

'Warm-hearted folk, the Geordies,' Culpeper suggested.

He watched Davidson with shrewd eyes. 'Anyway, tell me about this missing lad, Mr Isaacson.'

Saul Davidson frowned and sipped his coffee. He grimaced at its heat. 'Not a great deal to tell you, really. A good background, an earnest student. He was doing research here, and he worked with me but I can't say we got to know each other too well.'

'But you knew about this obsession of his.'

'Obsession. Yes, I suppose it's fair to call it that.' Davidson nodded thoughtfully, eyes averted. 'He had been told by his father about a man called Otto Wenschoff. He wanted to trace him. It's why he chose Newcastle as his university — he'd somehow found what he thought was a north-eastern connection.'

'And had he? Found a real connection, I mean?' Davidson shrugged non-committally. 'I can't say.'

'Did you have any personal involvement in this search of his?'

Davidson shook his head. 'Not really. Wasn't any of my business — nothing to do with me. I suppose I helped him to a certain extent. But as his tutor I advised him against spending too much time on it. Things like that, they can be self-destructive. You can have a dream, and it might turn sour.'

'How do you mean?' Culpeper asked.

'Well, the fact is Alex Isaacson wanted to find the man who saved his father — he was looking for a saint. But there are no saints, not really. There are only men and women, and they are made up of various emotions, and can behave in ways that are sometimes out of character. We're all flawed. We can do things which are . . . irrational. The man he sought had been a guard at the concentration camp at Auschwitz,

128

and apparently had behaved with humanity towards Alex Isaacson's father. But he was still a *guard* and maybe he had done other, unspeakable things too. That could have been what Isaacson would have discovered. Looking for a saint, finding a sinner. Such an experience could be shattering.'

'You warned him of this?'

'I did.'

'So what help did you actually give him, in his quest?'

Davidson considered the matter for a moment, then shook his head slowly. 'Nothing, really. Not to any great extent. The suggestions I made . . . they really led nowhere.'

'But why didn't you help him seriously?'

Professor Davidson seemed surprised at the question. He raised his quizzical eyebrows, a sadness in his pouched brown eyes. 'I've explained. I didn't really approve of the search he was conducting.'

'But you *could* have helped him, surely. A man of your background.'

Saul Davidson stiffened slightly and raised his head. His glance had sharpened, and Culpeper thought he detected a shadow of wariness in his manner: old instincts, he guessed, coming to the surface.

'What do you mean?' Davidson asked.

Culpeper smiled vaguely, rose from his chair and began a casual tour of the study. He looked along the line of books on the shelves, noting their archaeological bias. He stood at the window, looking out at pigeons strutting on the roofs above. He glanced at the papers littering Davidson's desk. The professor said nothing, but watched him carefully.

'You're already aware we found remains of a human body in the sea cave,' Culpeper stated.

'Old bones, I understand.'

'Depends what you mean by old. Some *very* old,' Culpeper asserted, 'some maybe twenty years old. And among those scattered bones we also picked up an identity disc. It belonged to a man called Winder.' He looked at Davidson. 'You ever heard of him?'

Davidson frowned, thinking; then he shrugged. 'I seem to have some recollection of the name, I think . . .'

'He worked on the railways. Disappeared, years ago. Reappeared, now. I wonder why you never told Alex Isaacson about him.'

'I had no special knowledge about this man Winder.'

'Now that surprises me, Professor Davidson. A man of your background, you'd have known all about Winder, wouldn't you? And maybe about Otto Wenschoff too. After all weren't they one and the same person? And didn't you know that?'

'Why should I be certain of such a thing?' Davidson countered evasively.

Culpeper gave a wolfish grin. 'Because of who you are, Professor Davidson, and what you've been.'

The ensuing silence grew around them like a muffling cloak.

2

The Assistant Chief Constable tapped an irritated pencil on the table in front of him in the conference room at Ponteland headquarters. He glared about him balefully. 'We really must get our priorities right,' he insisted.

The men seated facing him waited: Farnsby, Culpeper, three senior officers from uniformed branch, a couple of sergeants.

'It's quite clear,' the Assistant Chief Constable continued, 'that the trouble that's been festering in the south, over this whole question of the location and care of illegal immigrants, is going to spread north.'

'I don't know why they don't just send the buggers back where they came from,' one of the sergeants muttered audibly.

'That's not policy,' the Assistant Chief Constable flashed. 'And it's not the law. These people have entered the country illegally — that we know. And I have some sympathy for the view you express. But the fact remains, having entered, these people are now claiming political asylum, and while they are waiting for their cases to be dealt with, or appeals against deportation being made, they have to be looked after. That's the law. And we're here to enforce the law — particularly when unruly mobs try to subvert the system we are enjoined to uphold!' He glared around the room, daring dissent. There was a subdued shuffling of feet, but no one spoke. He turned to Farnsby. 'Uniformed branch are setting up the necessary precautions, but what have you been able to discover, Inspector Farnsby?'

Culpeper shifted his bulk uneasily on his narrow, uncomfortable chair as Farnsby began. He hoped he wouldn't go on too long.

'I've been busy co-ordinating the information that's been coming in from other police forces up and down the country,' Farnsby stated with an air of pompous confidence. 'From the intelligence coming in, it seems that this is to be a concerted day of action. It's being co-ordinated through certain web sites on the Internet, and though code names are being used we're pretty certain we are able to identify most of the ringleaders — not all, of course. One of them is in this area and is a man well known to us from past activities. Sid Larson.'

That old bugger still at it, Culpeper thought. Though it was surprising that he'd graduated to the Internet.

'What is clear,' Farnsby continued, 'is that we can expect co-ordinated outbreaks of staged, supposedly non-violent demonstrations at key points around the country. These will naturally be located near to the hot spots, if I may so describe them — those areas where illegal immigrants are presently being housed. Throughout the country—'

'We're not really interested in the rest of the country,' the Assistant Chief snorted impatiently, glancing at his watch, 'so let's concentrate on the northern area.'

Slightly ruffled, Farnsby continued. 'I've been in close and continuous contact with the designated liaison officers in the other northern forces, of course, sir. What we can expect to see is a series of demonstrations. For maximum effect they will be held in centres of significant population where they can occasion major disruption, rather than in the actual locations where immigrants are being held. There

132

will be a recognizable proximity, of course, to identify the rationale behind the demonstration—'

Culpeper yawned. The Assistant Chief Constable glared at him sourly.

'The centres which are currently being targeted — and where, naturally, the police forces will be concentrating are in Carlisle, York, Middlesbrough, Durham, Newcastle and, which affects us particularly, Alnwick.'

Culpeper grunted. 'So we can't expect to be able to draft coppers in from the other forces then.'

'That's correct,' Farnsby agreed stiffly. 'They'll have their own patches to protect. But at least we can pull in from throughout the county, since it seems that it is in Alnwick that the only demonstration within our jurisdiction will be held. We would have expected the demo to be at Morpeth, but it seems our demonstration is directed at that enclave of illegal immigrants who are currently being housed near Abbey village—'

'Bloody crazy place to hold them, if you ask me,' Culpeper offered.

Farnsby ignored him. '—and since Alnwick is the nearest centre of any size to that group, that's where the activists will gather. The demonstration is planned to take place on market day in the town, and it is likely that we can expect trouble, because it seems some of these illegal immigrants have started selling goods from makeshift stalls in the town on that day.'

'Even grunts have to live,' one of the sergeants conceded.

'Quite so,' Farnsby suggested, 'but it does raise certain dangers. A crowded marketplace, the presence of illegals, a demonstration that is more than likely to be infiltrated by unruly elements . . . We will need all the manpower that can be raised for the day, sir, and we will need a structured battle plan—'

Culpeper snorted derisively.

Farnsby swallowed hard. 'I've been in discussion with uniformed branch, and I understand they have already made contingency plans . . .'

He turned to the greying man in uniform seated to his left. The Assistant Chief Constable nodded. 'Superintendent Rogers.'

Culpeper listened half-heartedly as Rogers explained how he intended to curtail the movements of the demonstrators. He had arranged for barriers to be erected and the officers would try to channel the demonstrators into side streets wherever possible, away from the castle and away from the main cobbled area where the market stalls would be erected. Culpeper's attention wandered, and his mind drifted back to his conversation with Saul Davidson, in the professor's room at Newcastle University.

The professor's lean features had been stony, as Culpeper explained.

'You see, Professor Davidson, an old copper like me, we're not like the other bright young sparks who come flashing into the police firmament these days. We're more set in our ways, we're plodders, we rely on memory and experience. And some of these experiences, they get stuck in your mind, particularly if they're kind of unusual, out of the normal run at the time . . . And when we identified this guy Winder as being the heap of bones in the sea cave, there was something that started niggling at the back of my mind. That, and your name . . . I had the feeling you and I might have met, years ago, but I couldn't place your face; yet your name seemed somehow familiar.' He'd shaken his head in mock despair. 'But how come I'd remember someone's name from so long ago? And a professor, at that! I've met so many people over the years, rogues, ponces, tearaways, villains — not to suggest you're one of any of them, Professor Davidson! No, it had to be because there was something special about your name. Something unusual connected with it.'

Saul Davidson had remained silent, but there was a slightly hunted look about him. He had put down his cup of coffee. It was cooling, disregarded.

'But for an old copper like me, if your memory proves tricky, there's only one answer. Start digging among the paper. Raid the old files. Look for something special. Maybe something that never got resolved — because that was perhaps the reason why your name stuck. So I dug and plodded and sneezed in the dust down there in archives. And finally I found it. A file. One with a special tag on it in my mind. The memory stuck with me because in that file there was the kind of information that I'd never come across before. Nor since, for that matter, because we don't get much *international* stuff popping up here in Northumberland and Newcastle. Other than the usual run of foreign villains, dealing in drugs and whores.'

Davidson's pouched eyes were wary, but he feigned indifference. 'You don't see me as a foreign villain, surely.' Culpeper grinned, savouring the moment.

'Naw, you were always one of the goodies, weren't you?'

There was a short silence, as Davidson digested the comment, chewed it over suspiciously in his mind. 'I'm flattered, but what exactly is that supposed to mean?'

'Well,' Culpeper confided, leaning forward and lowering his voice in mock dramatics, 'I started by chasing up the old files for mention of Arthur Winder, and guess what? I found something, eventually. And then, guess what? Right slam bang in a connected file, marked *Secret* for God's sake, was a report from Special Branch! Can you believe it? A file marked *Secret* in our dusty old file system!'

'I wouldn't know whether that was unusual or not,' Davidson replied drily.

'Believe me, it is,' Culpeper breathed. 'But something else too — it's why my memory got triggered. Your name was in that file.'

Davidson made no comment, but his shoulders were rigid with a sudden tension.

'Don't you want to know why your name was in that file?'

'I'm sure you're going to tell me,' Davidson replied almost wearily.

Culpeper grinned in triumph. 'Correct, bonny lad. Your name was in there, in a Special Branch file, because at that time it was suspected that you were an agent acting on behalf of Israeli Secret Intelligence.'

Saul Davidson had then remained silent for a long while. At last he had opened the drawer of his desk and extracted a cigarette. 'I really must give these up,' he muttered disgustedly. But the first draw on the cigarette seemed to relax him. He breathed out gustily and nodded. 'Interesting . . . but old hat, I'm afraid. It's so long ago, now, I suppose there's no harm in admitting it, or talking about it.'

'I was hoping you'd feel that way,' Culpeper admitted affably.

'You probably didn't know what it was like in those days,' Davidson said. 'You'd be a young policeman, doing your normal job, policing the streets . . . It was different for me. A Jew, brought up in the States, seen as bright and intelligent . . . I was recruited by Mossad quite early in my career. Trained in Switzerland. Encouraged to locate in England and work undercover. But you know, Mr Culpeper, the initial excitement at being recruited into intelligence work soon drained away. First, because of the fact there was so little to do. I was really what they call a sleeper.'

Culpeper nodded. 'Not much espionage or mayhem in the northern pit villages. Except when Newcastle play Sunderland.'

Davidson smiled thinly. 'And then, I got immersed in my work at the university. I had been recruited and trained but life moved on . . . and then I received certain instructions. Regarding a man called Otto Wenschoff.'

'I thought as much.' Culpeper nodded.

'Agents had been tracing his career. He was small fry but still wanted for war crimes. Israeli agents had tracked him down to England, after the war, but it was difficult — the British authorities were alarmingly lax in 1945, and allowed all sorts of people in with false papers — Serbs, Romanians, Greeks, Italians, gipsies, drifters from war ravaged Europe. And once here, they virtually vanished with their new identities and new lives. But Wenschoff, he hadn't hidden too well. He was traced. They told me to check on him. He was calling himself Arthur Winder. I did so.'

'And the newspapers got hold of the story.'

Davidson nodded wearily. 'It was . . . leaked to them. The fact is, we wanted Wenschoff back for trial, but the evidence was a bit thin, and we weren't able to persuade Special Branch to co-operate with us. And we didn't want to effect a snatch in a foreign country. You'll recall what happened in the Eichmann affair: loud complaints and bad international publicity, even if we did bring a killer to justice.'

'You were responsible for the leak?'

Davidson hesitated, as though reluctant to admit to it.

Then he nodded, grudgingly. 'I was under instructions. The idea was by exposing the presence of an ex-SS man in Newcastle we'd raise a storm of protest put pressure on Special Branch, and get a popular demand for an investigation, his return . . . And the newspapers did in fact go to town, for a very brief while. But it never got the coverage that we'd expected. The timing was bad: the streets were being invaded by demonstrations, the miners' strike, struggles with authority, you remember how it went.'

Culpeper remembered. He had linked arms with colleagues in Northumberland and County Durham, and faced spitting women and frustrated men armed with wooden staves, men with whose cause he had much sympathy.

'And then Winder disappeared. Completely. And that was that. Except . . .' Saul Davidson hesitated. 'Except the incident had an effect on me. The newspapers had started to hound the man, even though they didn't have the evidence we had, and God knows that was thin enough. It was going to be a witch hunt. The fact it never became a *cause célèbre* was an accident — other news breaking, of more local importance. Violence in the streets. But Arthur Winder's life would have been ruined. And probably was ruined. But what if we had been wrong? What if Winder really wasn't Otto Wenschoff? Our evidence could have been flawed . . .' He inspected the glowing end of his cigarette and then, with a grunt of distaste, ground it out in the ashtray on his desk. 'The experience . . . my first real taste of activity . . . it left a sour taste in my mouth . . . disillusioned me. I resigned.'

'I didn't think that was possible,' Culpeper said.

'If you're sufficiently unimportant, it's possible,' Davidson assured him. 'And after that, I became just what I've remained — a professor at a university.'

'Until Alex Isaacson turned up, trying to find out about Wenschoff.' Culpeper eyed Saul Davidson with a degree of cynical disbelief. 'You could have told him what you've told me.'

'He wasn't a policeman. Just a misguided young man with a dream. And it was all so long ago. I tried to warn him off . . .'

'Was it you sent him to Bristol?'

Davidson shook his head. 'No, he found that link himself. It wasn't one I knew.'

'So you've no idea why the Bristol contact — Svensson would have advised him to talk to the owner of Abbey Manor?'

There was the briefest of hesitations, as though he was about to say something, then as he thought better of it Davidson shook his head. His glance was lowered, and he seemed to be churning something over in his mind. But when he looked up at Culpeper his eyes were deliberately guileless. 'I've no idea at all.'

Culpeper had observed him closely for a little while. He felt the man was lying — Davidson would have been trained to dissemble, but that would have been a long time ago. He sighed. 'So now, after all this time, what do you think? Arthur Winder . . . was he really Otto Wenschoff?'

Davidson's brown eyes had been uninterested. He shrugged. 'After all this time . . . who knows?'

It was unsatisfactory, and it hadn't got Culpeper any closer to finding out what had happened to Alex Isaacson.

The Assistant Chief Constable's voice brought him out of his reverie. 'I trust you're still with us, Culpeper!'

A sergeant snickered behind him. Culpeper shook himself. 'Of course, sir.'

'I'm just raising the question about priorities again. I'm told you've managed to keep yourself away from getting involved in this illegal immigrant issue. I would have thought a man like yourself, who takes pride in having an ear on the street, would have found this exactly the situation where you could provide real assistance. Talk to people. Find out what's going on. Who's likely to be involved, locally. What the reaction is to these allegations of rape, for instance.'

'Sir?'

Farnsby turned his saturnine features towards Culpeper. There was a gleam of superiority in his eyes as he picked up the surprise in Culpeper's voice. 'We've had a report in from Alnwick. A girl is claiming she was subjected to a rape.'

'Sally Armstrong,' someone muttered behind Culpeper. 'Well known to the lads.'

Farnsby ignored the comment. 'She claims rape. Two men of foreign origin, she says, couldn't speak English very well.'

'They didn't understand it when she said no,' Superintendent Rogers suggested, and one of the sergeants snickered sycophantically.

'We're calling a line-up of some of the illegals, to see if she can identify them,' Rogers added, 'but this girl, she's well known around about, and there's some doubt . . . Anyway, it's causing a lot of chat in the town. And maybe it'll have an effect on the demonstrators. Give them something to use, something else to start kicking about. I mean it's one thing to take our handouts and our jobs, but leave our whores alone. That sort of thing.'

'Culpeper?' The Assistant Chief Constable raised his eyebrows interrogatively.

'I been concentrating on other things, sir.'

'Such as?'

'Dead man in a cave,' someone behind Culpeper giggled.

The room was full of jokers, Culpeper thought sourly. 'We've identified the remains in the cave as probably those of a man called Arthur Winder, who disappeared twenty years or so ago.'

'And this is a *priority*?' the Assistant Chief Constable asked in disbelief. 'Is there evidence of foul play?'

Foul play. Christ, Culpeper muttered under his breath, is this a 1920s radio programme? 'We can't ascertain the exact cause of death, but a preliminary report from Forensic suggests Winder might have been injured, or killed, in a struggle. Damage to the skull. Of course, it's also possible the damage to the bones occurred in a fall down into the crevice on Abbey Head, so tests are still ongoing—'

'I see, so far, no reason why you're spending valuable time on this matter,' the Assistant Chief Constable stated icily. A hostile silence enveloped the room.

Culpeper tried to explain it to him later, in a private interview in the Assistant Chief Constable's office, after the meeting in the conference room had broken up. 'It's just that I have this feeling about it,' he said.

'*Feeling*.'

'Winder was being harassed, twenty years ago. He disappeared. He now turns up dead. Then a young man called Alex Isaacson starts looking for Otto Wenschoff—'

'You're losing me, Culpeper,' the Assistant Chief Constable warned.

'I think Arthur Winder was originally known as Otto Wenschoff, a guard at Auschwitz. Anyway, Winder disappears, Alex Isaacson turns up—'

'Twenty years later.'

'And he disappears.'

'So?'

'Isaacson was advised against seeking out Winder, advised by Saul Davidson, the man who originally shopped Winder to the press, years ago. Acting on instructions from Mossad.'

'What?' The Assistant Chief's tone exemplified incredulity. Culpeper ploughed on doggedly.

'But Isaacson managed to find his own contact in Bristol — a man who had known Winder up here in the north and this man, Svensson, he tells Isaacson that he'll get information from the owner of Abbey Manor.'

'Who is?'

'Hall Gabriel.' Culpeper hesitated. 'That's where there was a small hiccup. The information I got relayed to me, it wasn't quite right. Svensson couldn't have been talking about Hall Gabriel because Gabriel only recently bought Abbey Manor. He must have been talking about the Gibbs family. But Daniel Gibbs — who sold the property to Hall Gabriel — he'd have been just a kid twenty years ago, so it can't have been him that Svensson was referring to. But whoever Svensson was talking about, he was suggesting answers lay at Abbey Manor, and then there's the unlikely coincidence that after all these years Arthur Winder has turned up, in a sea cave at the edge of Abbey Manor property. I got a feeling the manor is central to the whole thing.'

There was a slightly glazed look in the Assistant Chief Constable's eyes.

'And then,' Culpeper confided, 'when I was up there at Abbey Manor, talking as it turned out to the wrong person, I got the feeling there was something odd going on. Gabriel admitted that Isaacson had been at the manor house. Said he'd turned him away, knew nothing about what the young man was on about. But then, Gabriel got quite shirty when I started asking questions. He wandered off at a tangent, claimed that someone's been skulking around the manor estate, and he showed me how his car had been damaged, but he doesn't want enquiries, wants to handle the matter himself—'

The Assistant Chief Constable gave up. He raised his hands. 'Enough, enough! Culpeper, just get on with this as quickly as you can. I don't want to hear anything more about it. But if you get nothing more concrete than this . . .' He struggled for words.

'Gut feeling,' Culpeper offered.

'Right. Gut feeling. If you have nothing better than that within twenty-four hours, I insist that you drop it. We've got too much on our plates, with the upcoming demonstrations, to spend valuable police time on gut feelings and twenty-year-old mysteries. We want *information* — so we can prepare for what we are pretty sure is coming.'

Culpeper returned in irritation to his office. Twenty-four hours — *balls*. He had lines of enquiry to follow and he wasn't going to be diverted from them. If he disobeyed the ACC, what were they going to do about it? Sack him? He was gone in a few weeks anyway. A suspension would only mean an earlier retirement, in effect.

He had the files on his desk: notes on the Winder affair at the time, stuffed in with accounts of the student riots, some scattered photographs, browning now with age. He glanced briefly at them, caught sight of someone who could have been a much younger Davidson. Maybe . . . *agent provocateur*, that one, for all that he now protested he was a small cog, low-key sleeper. Another young, vaguely familiar face, in the front row of a shouting, pushing mob. Strange . . . he wondered whether they had been misfiled. What did Winder have to do with student riots?

The second file was the Special Branch file, in which there were notes on Davidson. Nothing much to go on. He sat back, thinking. Culpeper felt certain that in some way Abbey Manor held the key to all this. And if it did, he'd better get as much information as he could on the previous owner of the estate.

Major Henry Gibbs.

And, he mused, while he was at it, he'd start a check running on Hall Gabriel as well, just for the hell of it.

And the ACC — he could get stuffed.

3

Karen Stannard walked across the beach towards Arnold, her hair blowing in the wind, the afternoon sun highlighting the line of her cheekbones. She walked with a long, swinging stride, almost like the model she could easily have been mistaken for. She was dressed in tight worn jeans, scuffed boots, and her blouse, open at her tanned throat, was covered by a light leather jacket that had seen better days. She was clearly not intending to go to the office this afternoon. This was site visiting, to check on Arnold Landon, he had no doubt.

'I've just been up at Roundsay and taken a look at what's going on up there,' she explained. 'Portia's got everything under control.' She eyed him carefully, as though expecting some reaction at the mere mention of her assistant's name. A little disappointed at his indifference, she went on, 'And now I thought I'd take another look at the famous sea cave. There's another do coming up, Arnold, and I'll want you there on the day.'

'What's happening?'

She planted her hands on her hips and breathed deeply, her breasts rising in spectacular fashion. She smiled at him, knowing the effect she could create in a man's mind and body. 'It's good to get out of the office, take in the sea breezes. I wouldn't mind changing my responsibilities for yours, Arnold.'

She was lying in her perfect teeth, he thought. She knew what he was thinking, and grinned tantalizingly. 'Anyway, the grant's been approved, cheques are to be handed over, and I've managed to obtain another sponsor a big building firm who want the limelight. It's all coming together, Arnold, and the big day will be next week, at Alnwick. I've arranged for a room booking at the White Swan in the main street. We should get the media to attend again — but it may be they're getting a bit of overkill from us with these announcements. So what we really need is something new we can throw at them. Hence, I'm here, to look over the possibilities. See if there isn't some new angle we can give them about the sea cave which will sharpen their interests, and their pencils. So, cup of coffee, or tea, first of all, whichever you can rustle up, and then I'd like you to give me a tour.'

She caught sight of Chris Hayman standing near the entrance to the sea cave, watching them. 'How's he getting on?' she asked, suspicion staining her tone.

'I'm trying to keep him busy,' Arnold explained. 'But it's not easy. I'm beginning to think it wasn't such a good idea, letting him join the team.'

'He seems to want to tag along with you.'

'I don't think he's ever made any friends in the department,' Arnold replied uneasily. 'And my guess is he's still not come to terms with his wife's suicide. There are times when he seems to lose himself, stare out to sea. He walked off without a word one afternoon, and I saw him up on the headland, near the abbey ruins, just standing there.'

'You think he's heading for a nervous breakdown?' Karen Stannard asked. There was a sudden concerned gentleness in her tone which made Arnold glance at her in surprise. She caught the glance, and regained control. 'If he's really got a problem, he should be put on sick leave.'

'I don't know that it's got as far as that,' Arnold muttered. 'And I don't think he'd welcome staying away from work, in an empty house.'

'But if working here isn't a suitable therapy . . .' she doubted. 'Well, keep an eye on him, and keep me informed.'

Arnold led the way to the hut, where he made her a cup of coffee while she leaned over the long table that had been erected to take the various artefacts the team had begun sifting from the cave floor. 'So what have we got here?' she asked, interest glowing in her face.

'It's quite a range,' Arnold suggested. 'The police activity in the cave made things very problematic for us, as you can imagine, but we've still managed to excavate a significant amount of material from the floor of the chamber. To begin with, there's a considerable amount of evidence of Celtic use. That piece of red glass there — you see it has the hint of a swastika pattern? Then there's a sliver of carved antler, which I think probably dates from the early first century. You remember those carvings lining the shaft at Fellbach-Schmiden, that were dated to 125 BC? I reckon this particular fragment here is very similar.'

'I see what you mean.' Karen Stannard leaned over the small objects, peering at them closely. 'Any pottery?'

'Several fragments. We know that the north was aceramic in the last pre-Christian centuries, but there are some pieces here that'd suggest material was brought in from other regions. There's some terracotta, a piece of what looks to me like a broken section of an ancient ornamental disc, or plate—'

'*Phalera*,' Karen murmured, in confirmation of his view.

'And there's some examples of ironwork. This I guess is a piece of a cart fitting; this I suspect to be a bit of a locally made iron sickle; and this a brooch section—'

'*Fibulae*,' she nodded. She took a deep breath, surveying the whole table. Then she moved around its length, looking closely at each item in the scattered collection, checking on the descriptive tags the team had added as the finds came to light. 'So, the Well of Time,' she murmured.

'That's right. People will have cast these into the shaft, if my theory is correct, though they might of course have been deposited in the cave when the entrance was open, a long time ago. There are a few small votive offerings as well, at the end of the table there. Arrow heads, a knife blade, a fertility symbol . . .'

'But you still think these would have been tossed into Hades Gate as offerings to the gods, for . . . how long?'

'Millennia,' Arnold guessed. 'And Professor Davidson suggests from his observations that the flying figures and the petroglyphs in the sea cave would presume a much older, shamanistic society, connected with chthonic beliefs . . .'

'Hades Gate, the entrance to the underworld.' Karen Stannard sighed, and shook her head. 'It's great stuff, Arnold, and it'll give us years of work, or at least, we'll get the universities involved—'

'Professor Davidson is enthusiastic.'

She nodded. 'It's great, and we can weave a good story around it for the press to write up, but I still think it's not *enough*. You know what I mean. We're in a competitive business. There are new finds cropping up all over the place: archaeology is suddenly fashionable, in the public consciousness. But if we're going to take advantage of that, seize the opportunity to get better funding rolling into the department, expand our activities—'

And her reputation, Arnold guessed.

'—we need to find something special. When we get this cheque handing-over ceremony at Alnwick, I'd love to be able to say we've found something really good. I mean, all this is admirable, but as you know, Arnold, it only matches finds elsewhere. Most of this is pretty common — there's nothing here that's really *spectacular*. That's what we need. Something that's going to catch the public imagination.'

'We can't find what's not there,' Arnold replied.

'But there's bound to be something! A ritual centre for millions of years — there's bound to be something. And you've been lucky enough in the past . . .'

She sipped at the coffee he had made for her and wandered around the table, eyeing the artefacts displayed there, muttering to herself occasionally, murmuring appreciation of some of the objects, holding them up, inspecting them. Arnold watched her, admiringly. He knew she was committed to her chosen career. He was aware that she was as obsessed with the past as he was, and he recognized that she possessed a deep understanding of the work in the field. And she was a beautiful woman.

The pity was that over all this lay a patina of ambition, a desire to never give way, an urgent need to win, even if it meant trampling on others. There was a streak of ruthlessness in Karen Stannard, but when she looked at a man, and the deep colours in her eyes changed . . .

She was staring at him. 'Daydreaming, Arnold?'

He was confused. 'Maybe when you've finished your coffee we should go into the sea cave. I understand what you've been saying, but I doubt if we'll be able to come up with anything of great assistance for your meeting at Alnwick. The press will have to be satisfied with what we've got. But—'

She nodded. 'Let's take a look in the cave.'

She put down her mug and led the way out into the hazy sunlight. A light sea fret was drifting in and in an hour or so Arnold guessed it would be damp to the skin, misty along the beach. As they approached the entrance Hayman came out, nodded briefly to them, and walked aimlessly across to the sea wall. Karen eyed him suspiciously. 'Where's he going now?'

Arnold shrugged. 'Working in the cave can be a bit claustrophobic. We all need to get out of there from time to time, get some air, get orientated again. In the darkness, with the flashlights, it can be oppressive.'

'You've got a generator. Why aren't you lighting up the cave completely?'

'Professor Davidson was against it. He's already concerned that with us working on the chamber floor as a group, damage could be taking place on the walls. The pigmentation could be affected by condensation from our breathing. Our body heat could affect the paintings; and using hot lights could make things even worse. So, I'm afraid it's still semi-darkness when we go in there.'

She looked back to Hayman. He was staring up at the sky, and the cliffs. His shoulders were tense, he seemed under some kind of strain. She shook her head. 'I think we'll have to bring him back into the office. He's not looking too good to me.'

Arnold was inclined to disagree. But it would be her decision, in the end.

He led the way into the sea cave.

The light was harsh just inside the entrance, where lighting equipment had been installed by one of the team, but as they edged their way past their colleagues, murmuring greetings, further into the cave it became more difficult to see clearly. Karen paused from time to time, shining her flashlight on the carvings, the footprints carved in the rock, the faintly discerned paintings of shamanistic flying men. 'They're almost modernistic, in their economy of line . . . Can we get photographs, Arnold?'

'Already done.'

'We'll get some blown up, use as a backdrop in our room at the hotel, when we meet the press. I'll get the PR department to come up with a design . . .'

Duckboards had been laid down the centre of the chamber. The team had been working with precision, sifting the material on the floor of the cave, marking the location of finds with care. The result was they had to step lightly, alert to the danger of disturbing anything. Karen's flashlight continued to probe at the walls and the roof. She switched off at one point, to approve of the dim bluish light that filtered through the gathering darkness in the depths of the chamber. 'It must have been a place of wonder to ancient men,' she breathed.

She stood there for a little while, contemplating it. The air was chill, and there was a little movement, a feather touch to their cheeks as they stood there, air moving down through the blow-hole. Karen lifted her head, switched her flashlight on again and gestured forward. 'Let's take another look at the rock fall.'

The police had worked in the area with an inevitable crudeness. Where the bones of Arthur Winder had been found they had scraped and shovelled out much of the stone and debris that had accumulated there. Once they had removed the remains of the skeleton, and stacked the rubble to one side, they had left the cave to the archaeologists, but the team had done little work there.

'There seemed little point,' Arnold explained. 'The first thing we needed to do was to make sure nothing else was damaged or lost. So the floor of the cave was the first priority, working inwards. As you'll have seen back there, a large part of the chamber has now been sifted, but they haven't reached as far in as this yet.' He flickered his own torch beam over the pile of rubble and stone that lay piled ahead of them, at the end of the lobed chamber. 'That's where we experienced the rock fall. And that's where I suspect is the chimney, that probably leads up to the cleft in the headland — Hades Gate.'

Karen nodded, and moved forward. She began to clamber over the pile of broken stone.

'Take care,' Arnold warned. 'I don't want to carry you out of here with a broken ankle.'

'Why? Because you'd have to manage the department? At least it would keep you out of fist fights!'

His bruises had disappeared, but she was not going to let him forget the fracas in Abbey village for a long time. She was scrambling up on to the pile of stones, gripping the rock face with her left hand, shining her flashlight about her, inspecting the rock. 'There's some pretty large stuff here,

Arnold, and it's going to take some moving. But my bet would be that we'd find something under here, once we've moved this rubble.'

'That'll take weeks.'

'I don't doubt it.' She turned her head. 'Here, give me a hand.'

Arnold stepped up behind her, balancing precariously on the rock. Some of the rubble moved under his feet, so when he grabbed at Karen's thighs it was as much to support himself as to lend her assistance. He was aware of the tensing of her thigh muscle under his hand. She looked back at him. He sensed a certain amusement in her tone. 'Don't take advantage of the situation, Arnold!'

She was leaning forward, straining upward, shining her flashlight above her. 'You're right, you know. There's a clear fissure here, there's no light but my bet is this could well lead up to the headland. If I can just reach up . . .'

She stepped up on the fallen stones, away from his supporting hands, until her head was hidden in the narrow chimney. 'I don't think this is a good idea,' Arnold suggested. 'You can't get far up anyway, and the headland must be more than a hundred feet above us. You can't—'

Next moment she was wriggling away from him, climbing into the shaft of the rock chimney, bracing her feet against the sides of the fissure. He heard her voice, already somewhat disembodied, producing an echo that skittered down into the chamber and faded against the dark walls. 'This is the advantage of keeping slim,' she announced. 'You can get into the most surprising places.'

He scrambled up a little way behind her, flashing his torch beam upwards. The entrance to the fissure was narrow enough, but some six feet above his head he could now see that it widened somewhat, and Karen was actually moving upwards into the darkness with a certain degree of ease, her own torch flashing on the walls above her head. She stopped for a few moments, and he could hear the quickness of her breathing from her exertions. She called back down to him.

'The chimney widens even more just above my head. There's a sort of protruding ledge, but from what I can see after that the fissure opens out considerably. I'll just try to see if I can reach . . .'

There was no point arguing with her. And she had been right — slimness was an advantage. The narrow aperture she had squeezed through would have been almost impossible for Arnold to manage. He could only wait, and make sure she didn't get into any difficulty.

'That's right,' he heard her pant, 'I think I can reach this ledge. Then if I can just pull myself up . . .'

There was a shower of small stones, dirt, soft material that skittered past him as he stood below her at the entrance to the fissure. He could see her legs, but not the upper part of her body as she scrambled further up into the shaft. She was kicking at the rock, trying to achieve a more secure foothold, and then he could hear her gasping at the exertion as she pulled herself up to the unseen ledge. Then, as Arnold flashed his torch up into the shaft, he could see her no more.

'Made it!' He heard her exclaim in triumph. She was panting hard, and the sound echoed down to him eerily, in the way the sounds from the blow-hole must have echoed up the shaft to Hades Gate for millennia. He waited, and he heard the sound of her scrabbling about on the ledge. Then she was silent.

'Karen?'

She made no reply, but he could see the torchlight wavering in the height of the fissure. It flashed about, uncertainly, and then seemed to fix on a particular point, trembling, shaking slightly. When she drew a sharp breath, the sound of the intake slivered down to the chamber below.

'Oh, my God!'

'Karen? What's happened?'

There was a short silence, and then, to his relief, she announced, 'I'm coming back down.'

He waited, he saw her swing her legs back down into the fissure above his head, lowering herself away from the rocky ledge. Small pieces of stone scattered about him as she scrabbled with her feet for purchase; at one point he thought she had lost her hold on the rock face and was swinging, almost falling, but then she obtained a grip again, coming down, gasping with the effort, until he was able to reach up, touch her ankle, help ease her down from the narrow fissure entrance, squeezing out again into the chamber itself.

When she finally dropped to the rock pile he caught her, his arms going around her. She leaned against him. He realized she was shaking. 'What's the matter?'

She stayed close to him for a moment, clinging, then she pulled away, stepping down from the rock pile to the floor of the cave. He dropped down beside her. In the reflected beam of his torch her features had lost their colour, and she appeared almost ethereal, strangely insubstantial. She was breathing hard, but she was regaining control of herself.

'I wanted something special to get the attention of the media at our ceremony,' she muttered grimly, 'but this isn't quite what I was looking for.'

A cold feeling crept through Arnold's veins. 'What's happened? What did you find up there?'

She took a deep, shuddering breath. 'Another bloody problem for us, Arnold, that's what. I touched it first, on the ledge, and then I . . . saw it.' Her eyes were deep hollowed in the reflected light. 'There's a dead man up there on the ledge.'

Inadvertently, taken aback, he glanced up into the shaft she had just left.

'But I'm not talking about old bones,' she muttered shakily. 'I mean . . . a dead man!'

CHAPTER FIVE

1

'Things look different now, don't they?' Culpeper announced almost triumphantly. Farnsby shuffled in discomfort as he stood in front of Culpeper's desk. Culpeper leaned back in his chair and locked his hands behind the back of his head. There was a beatific smirk on his face.

When the news had come in, everything had changed, and there was no more talk of priorities from the Assistant Chief Constable. Culpeper had demanded Farnsby's assistance immediately and together they had gone out to the sea cave. It had soon become apparent that access to the ledge where Karen Stannard had found the body would be difficult so it had been decided that a team should attempt access from Hades Gate. It had proved possible: the fissure was some eight feet wide in places and plunged vertically, twisting erratically into the cliff; men with the appropriate experience were drafted in and the descent was made. A winch was erected on the edge of the ancient fissure, the whole area roped off and Culpeper had watched the operation go forward. He had already spoken at length to both Karen Stannard and Arnold Landon, and it was with some satisfaction that he had launched Farnsby on to a series of investigations.

It took a little time, but once the team leader was down in the fissure the body was finally recovered from the crevice and the ledge surprisingly quickly. Culpeper had never heard of anyone venturing into Hades Gate previously. It was possible that its evil reputation, and the strange sounds that had emanated from it over the centuries, had built some kind of aura of danger about it that had deterred anyone from attempting to enter it. Now that it had been entered, he had no doubt potholing teams would visit the site with regularity — provided they obtained permission from the owner of the land, Hall Gabriel.

Gabriel. The man was on Culpeper's list.

He eyed Inspector Farnsby with a satisfied gleam in his eye. 'All right, bonny lad. Tell me what you got.'

'First, we now have absolute confirmation that the body found was that of Alex Isaacson. Second, we have yet to get a complete report from the pathology labs but we certainly can't rule out murder. The neck was broken, the skull partly crushed: the thought is it could be possible that he had simply fallen and injured himself—'

'But he'd been up to Abbey Manor and was looking for Arthur Winder and would hardly have thrown himself down into Hades Gate on that quest,' Culpeper commented sarcastically. 'Even if he'd known he was there.'

Farnsby nodded. 'I think we need to proceed on the assumption that violence was involved. Now, you suggested that we do a quick check on what we can discover about Isaacson's whereabouts and movements, after he returned north. His friends at the digs he stayed at including the young girl you interviewed, sir — are all adamant that they never saw him after his return. On the other hand, Hall Gabriel and his . . . right-hand man, Sean Corman, they admit that Isaacson did in fact turn up at Abbey Manor. And we have another sighting, later that Saturday evening. It seems that Isaacson stopped off at the pub in Abbey village.'

'By himself?'

'He wasn't alone.'

'Any description of the man who was with him?'

'Bit vague, sir. But the barman thought it was the man who started that fracas a few weeks back, over the illegal immigrants.'

Culpeper grimaced. 'My old friend, Sid Larson. Interesting . . . What would he be doing with Isaacson?' He frowned, thinking for a little while as Farnsby waited patiently. 'And after this pub meeting?'

Farnsby shook his head. 'Nothing. No sighting. The two men left, together, it seems.'

'And their behaviour, in the pub?'

'Deep in conversation, it seems. Not a casual chat. Serious.'

Culpeper sighed, unlocked his fingers and flexed them. 'All right . . . keep trying to find out if there have been any other sightings of the pair after the meeting in the pub. And we'd better haul in Sid Larson immediately for questioning.'

Farnsby met his eyes directly. 'I've already spoken with him, sir. He says he has an alibi for the relevant time. Reckons he was drinking with his mates at the Labour Club.'

'That bloody mob of his would back each other up in hell,' Culpeper sneered. 'Check it out — but my guess is there'll be big holes in that alibi.'

Farnsby nodded, then consulted his notebook. 'Then there's the matter of the owner of the Abbey Manor estate. Hall Gabriel.'

'Almost the last person to see Isaacson alive. Tell me.'

'He says he remained at the manor that evening: didn't go out. He's backed by Sean Corman.'

'His strong-arm man would obviously back him up.'

'And when we were talking to Gabriel, he started arguing about being persecuted again. He told you about the damage to his cars. He now says that Corman's patrolling the woods at night, to try to catch the guy who's victimizing him.'

'I wouldn't like to be the person caught by Corman in the dark,' Culpeper suggested. 'I can guess very clearly why

Gabriel employs him. And it's not to tuck him up in bed at night with a stiff whisky. But what about Gabriel himself — what have you dug up about him generally?'

Farnsby shrugged, and grimaced. 'Not a great deal, for such a public man. I mean, the usual stuff about a rise to riches and fortune, but his origins are not well detailed. We do know that he was brought up here in the north-east, and has returned to his roots, though he doesn't seem to me to be the sentimental kind who would be motivated like that. He started a small transport business with a man called Angell that's well enough documented — and it was pretty shaky for a while. A few school bus contracts, the odd haulage deal. But it was no great shakes, and at some point he bought out his partner, though rumour has it there was something a bit iffy about it, after which the business seems to have expanded rapidly, property development as well as transport, and he moved south — and things went well for him thereafter. Europe was the making of him. Long haul stuff, rapid turnover, expanding transport fleet. But it all runs itself now, and he claims he wants to enjoy some leisure up here in the north. Loves the countryside, he says.'

Culpeper sniffed doubtfully. 'No, I suspect there's more to it than that. And anything about this stalker he's shouting about?'

Farnsby shook his head. 'I guess there is someone with a grudge, but it might be just about the flashy cars Gabriel has. We've no leads, that's for sure.'

'Well, keep digging,' Culpeper ordered. 'I don't like Gabriel — too smooth, too arrogant. And I'm not entirely convinced that he knows nothing about Isaacson. You've spoken again to Professor Davidson?'

'We told him about finding Isaacson's body,' Farnsby replied. 'And he seemed shaken. But he's a very controlled man, isn't he, sir? He sort of clammed up when I tried to find out more about his relationship with Isaacson. I'm beginning to feel he isn't telling us everything he knows about this whole business of Winder, Wenschoff and Isaacson.'

'I think you're right.' Culpeper scratched at his jaw thoughtfully. 'We need to keep close tabs on our ex-Mossad agent, Professor Saul. What was he up to that Saturday night when we know Isaacson visited Gabriel at Abbey Manor?'

Farnsby's features were expressionless. 'At home. Alone. Except for a bottle of whisky.'

'No wife, or girlfriend to confirm it?'

Farnsby shook his head. 'Confirmed bachelor, Professor Davidson. But . . . there's something bothering him, something gnawing at him, I'm certain.'

Culpeper felt the same way. He looked at Farnsby reflectively. Maybe the younger man would make a decent copper yet. Hard work was essential, but so were gut feelings — provided you didn't rely too much on them to jump to early conclusions. But, he agreed, something was indeed gnawing at Professor Davidson, but whether it was about Isaacson, or something that happened twenty years ago . . . 'All right, so where does that leave us?'

Farnsby shrugged helplessly. 'No direct leads, really. A lot of questions, but I can't yet see any links anywhere.'

Culpeper considered the matter as the silence lengthened around them. At last, he said, 'Well, first of all, we've got Sid Larson. We have a witness to say he was with Isaacson in that pub on Saturday night. We have Gabriel admitting to seeing Isaacson earlier, and we have Sean Corman scuffling around in the undergrowth looking for the odd break-and-enter merchant. We have friend Davidson muttering into his cocoa about something that's bothering him, but he's keeping his mouth shut so far . . . All right, let's keep niggling at this. I want pressure on Davidson. I want to find out more about Gabriel, especially about the way he got started in business; and I want Larson in here for questioning. Alibi be buggered, I want to have a go at him personally. It will give me pleasure.'

'There's one other person to talk to, sir. He's been away from the area the last few days, but we've contacted him again now.'

Culpeper raised his eyebrows.

'Daniel Gibbs,' Farnsby explained. 'He's agreed to come in this afternoon.'

'The man Gabriel bought Abbey Manor from . . . All right, I'll see him myself. Before I get my teeth into the thuggish Sid Larson.'

* * *

Daniel Gibbs was clearly nervous. Some people were naturally concerned merely at being faced by a copper in an interview room. Culpeper had known it seize a man's vocal cords in a strangling grip, cause a man's whole body to break out into an uncontrolled sweat. With Gibbs it was a hunted look, eyes seeming restless, shooting glances all around the room, anywhere but towards the man facing him. Culpeper didn't mind such reactions, they could help. They sometimes made a man indiscreet.

'So, Mr Gibbs,' Culpeper asked in a jovial tone. 'Down south on business?'

Gibbs swallowed hard, trying to keep the tremor out of his voice. 'Not really, Chief Inspector. As you know, I recently sold Abbey Manor. There were a lot of bills to pay, but at the end of it all, I've got a reasonable amount of money, and I've been seeking advice on its investment. So, partly to see my brokers, partly just to . . . chill out, sort of.'

Culpeper thought that Gibbs was wishing he could chill out, as he put it, right now.

'So, how long have you been down there . . . London, was it?'

'That's right. About a week.'

'And you've heard about the discovery of Alex Isaacson's body in Hades Gate, of course.'

'Dreadful business.'

'Did you know him?'

Gibbs shook his head, a little too emphatically. 'No, never.'

'No contact with him of any kind?'

'None.'

'So why would he have been coming to see you at Abbey Manor, the day he died?' Culpeper asked pleasantly.

'Was he?' There was an attempt to inject surprise in the tone, but it was overlaid by something else. Gibbs blinked hard. 'Look, I'm not sure what you mean, but I didn't know this man, and . . . do you think I should have a solicitor present?'

'Do *you* think so?' Culpeper countered. After a short, edgy silence, he leaned forward, linked his fingers together and smiled at Gibbs. 'Look here, son, let me put the cards on the table. We know that Alex Isaacson had been probing into the history of an Auschwitz guard called Otto Wenschoff. It seems Wenschoff ended up here in the north, calling himself Arthur Winder. Isaacson goes down to Bristol meets an old man called Svensson who knew Winder, and as a result he gets advised to go talk to someone in Abbey Manor. We've checked with Mr Gabriel — he says he met Isaacson but didn't know what the hell he was on about. So, maybe it wasn't Hall Gabriel that Isaacson was supposed to meet. Maybe Svensson had advised him to talk to you — the owner before Gabriel.'

Daniel Gibbs licked his lips. 'Why don't you ask this man Svensson about it?'

Culpeper sighed. 'We would have done. But he was an old man. He died in the nursing home. A week ago. When you were in London, I suppose.' He raised interrogative eyebrows. 'So, was it you who Isaacson wanted to talk to?'

'He would have no reason to. He wouldn't know me. But . . . maybe it was my father he was seeking.'

'Your father's been dead for years, son.'

'Yes, but this man Svensson,' Gibbs replied earnestly, 'if he's been living in Bristol for some time, and he's an old man, he could have been confused, sent Isaacson back north to Abbey Manor to speak to my father. He wouldn't know about the major's death.'

'The *major*?'

'My father. Major Henry Gibbs. He was in the army. Had some bad experiences. Maybe that was what it was all about.'

The words had come out in an urgent rush, fear pumping adrenaline into Daniel Gibbs's veins. Culpeper watched him carefully for a little while. 'Maybe you'd better tell me about your father, Mr Gibbs.'

Floodgates suddenly opened. Culpeper sat quietly and listened as he heard the story of a boy who had never been close to his father, who had respected him but feared him also, not because of any violence shown to him as a child, but for the distant, cold, strict Victorian paterfamilias attitude Henry Gibbs had adopted towards his only son. He'd seen very little of him during his formative years, as the son recalled, and Daniel had broken away to build his own life, but he had been forced to come back to the manor when his father died. When he explained what had happened, Culpeper raised his shaggy eyebrows.

'Suicide?'

Gibbs shrugged. 'The coroner merely gave the usual verdict — "when the balance of his mind was disturbed".'

'You've no idea what it was about?'

Gibbs shook his head. 'I don't know. But I've always suspected it might have been something to do with his experiences in the army.'

Culpeper frowned. 'And what were they?'

'Court-martialled. Dishonourable discharge.'

The silence grew around them, miserably, as Daniel Gibbs seemed to shrink in his chair, shamed for the shame his father had carried.

'What were the circumstances?' Culpeper asked.

Gibbs grimaced. 'He never really talked about it. I don't know the full story. And I've never read the official account of the proceedings against him. But I think it was something to do with a prisoner of war. In 1945.'

'How do you mean?'

Gibbs raised his head. His eyes were vague, hints of an old anguish in their depths. 'I think my father shot him. While the man was unarmed, and in custody.'

Culpeper drummed his fingers on the table in front of him. Outside the room he heard steps proceeding along the corridor; they faded. Outside the narrow window of the interview room a blackbird burst into song from the cherry trees across the lawns. A prisoner of war. Shot while in custody. A court martial. A dishonourable discharge. The army would have records, but it was a long time ago, and the Ministry of Defence, it was never all that keen to dig out for public scrutiny records of such ancient offences. Particularly if they reflected badly in any way upon the service.

'What sort of war did your father have?' Culpeper enquired curiously.

'What he told me about, he seemed pretty proud of,' Gibbs replied. 'He landed in Italy, served in the Intelligence Corps, saw action and was wounded slightly. And . . .' He hesitated. 'I believe he ended up in the Carinthians. Which is where it happened.'

'The shooting.'

'Yes.'

'Do you know why he shot this prisoner of war?' Gibbs shook his head. 'He never told me. Said nothing about the incident. But you see, Mr Culpeper, after he was discharged, I think he became a bitter man. He felt it had been an injustice, his discharge. He had served his country and now he had been dishonoured. It was why he clung to his rank — major. It was like an act of defiance. But I think his views became soured, twisted.'

'How do you mean?'

'He was filled with hate. For all sorts of things.'

'Just because of his discharge?'

'No, not just that.' Gibbs looked round the room, clearly troubled at being asked to peel back the layers that would have surrounded his father, motives, views, events that

162

made up his soured character, feelings that led him to take his own life. 'No, I think it was because of what he saw.'

'How do you mean?'

Daniel Gibbs frowned. 'He visited the death camps. He entered Treblinka, to interrogate officers there. And from there he went to the Carinthian mountains.'

'I thought you said he didn't tell you about all this,' Culpeper asked wonderingly.

'He didn't.' Gibbs twisted awkwardly in his chair. 'He never really said very much at all. But after he died, I came home, and I had to sort through his things. There was some pretty pornographic stuff there.'

Culpeper's eyes widened. 'Obscenities?'

Gibbs shook his head violently. 'No, not that kind of thing. Hate. Twisted views of mankind. The things that should be done to the people he hated. He was a supporter of extreme right-wing organizations. He took their literature. He even founded his own organization up here in the north: Sons of England.'

'Anti-Semitic?'

'No, not that.' Gibbs was struggling to find the right words. 'He saw England as in some way pure. And he had tried to protect it, and had suffered from it. That was the injustice. And he poured out his feelings in an attitude towards other races, those who had been involved in the conflict in the 1940s. The stuff he had, the Sons of England material, it was awful; obscene. I burned it. We were never that close, but I wouldn't have wanted it to become public knowledge, the kind of man he had become.'

'So what did you do?' Culpeper asked gently.

'Burned most of it. Destroyed it in a bloody great bonfire.'

Culpeper was silent for a while, watching Gibbs thoughtfully. Links in a chain . . . 'Do you think your father might ever have met Otto Wenschoff?'

'Who?'

The ignorance was real. Culpeper was silent again.

Something was puzzling him. 'You say you burned *most* of your father's stuff. Did you keep any of it?'

Gibbs hesitated, then nodded. 'There was something. A manuscript. I found it locked away in my father's desk. I tried reading it once, but it was painful. I think he intended to try to get it published one day, maybe as an explanation, a rationale for his behaviour at the end of the war. I don't know. I never finished reading it. The manuscript itself, it was never finished, in fact.' He shrugged despondently. 'I didn't have the heart to destroy it. Because, in a sense, it was an historical document.'

'So where is it now?'

'I thought it best to make sure it was preserved somewhere . . . as a relic of the war. In an academic environment. I donated it to the university archives.'

'Which university?'

'Newcastle.'

'And to whom did you give it?' Culpeper asked, a slow suspicion turning over in his mind.

'One of the professors there. He knew a great deal about the war.'

'Professor Saul Davidson?'

Daniel Gibbs's eyes widened. 'How did you know that?'

2

The distant, discordant drumming could be heard faintly in the conference room where a small group of journalists from local newspapers and television had gathered, to be greeted with glasses of wine and thin sandwiches, fruit, cakes and assorted biscuits. Arnold stood leaning against the wall near the window, keeping himself in the background as he watched Karen, formally attired in white blouse and dark grey suit, moving easily amongst the guests, laughing lightly from time to time, greeting a familiar face here, shaking hands with a newcomer, generally demonstrating to everyone that this was her day and she was in charge.

Arnold was the only other person present from the department. He had expected that Karen would have arranged for Portia Tyrrel to be available for the meeting also, but he guessed she had thought that would be overegging the pudding. One beautiful woman was enough, particularly if Karen wanted to be entirely the centre of attention. And she was certainly that.

He had had some difficulty reaching the White Swan earlier that afternoon. Driving into Alnwick had been something of a nightmare. The queues of vehicles waiting to move into the narrow gateway to the town from the south had stretched back up the hill, way past the monument with its proud-tailed Percy lion. Time had ticked away as Arnold waited impatiently, with the traffic edging forward only feet at a time. When he reached Bondgate he realized the delay was due to a police presence, rerouting traffic across to the left, away from the centre of town. A demonstration was planned, it seemed. The polite young police constable he spoke to told him if he parked in a side street on the hill he would be able to walk down to the hotel through one of the narrow ginnels that ran into the town itself.

He did as was suggested, found a parking place outside a private house — hoping he'd not be meeting an irate house-holder later — and walked down to the first of the barriers erected along the town entrances.

The situation was exacerbated by the fact it was market day in Alnwick and a considerable number of stalls had been erected where vendors were selling a range of articles from scrubbing brushes to kiwi fruits, bottles of bleach to joggers, trainers and waterproof, thornproof waxed jackets. There was a considerable hubbub, a few placards to be seen, but at that point it seemed that the police precautions had discountenanced the demon-strators who had been expecting to take over the town centre. There were a few to be seen, waving their arms and chanting, but Arnold was aware of a vague drifting of people in the side streets and the narrow road leading up to Alnwick Castle.

He barely managed to make it to the hotel in time. When he entered the conference room, Karen caught sight of him, came across and hissed, 'Are you *ever* on time?'

He didn't bother to explain — she would know the problem anyway, had probably run the gauntlet herself, and was merely letting off steam. She enjoyed these public appearances, but he suspected there were always underlying nerves she fought to control, in spite of her public demon-stration of ease, friendliness and assurance.

'Where did you manage to park your car?' he asked.

'I got the last place in the hotel car park,' she replied. 'Anyway, let's get on . . .'

The media presence was better than they might reasonably have expected, but Arnold noted the way in which several of the newspaper people tended to stroll across to the windows, to look outside to the market square. They were checking if there might be something more exciting to report in the street outside, and Arnold had the feeling that if any spurt of activity did occur, the conference room in the hotel would very quickly be abandoned.

But for the moment, all was well, and Karen was introducing her new sponsor, a middle-aged, muscular man with a bald head and an off-the-peg crumpled check suit that loudly proclaimed he was a self-made man who'd come up the hard way in the building trade and he wasn't going to put on any airs, even if he was pumping a lot of money into this project. Arnold noted he had a pint of beer in his ham fist, specially brought in for him, while the rest of the people in the room drank wine or orange juice. It was, he supposed, by way of making a statement.

After a short delay Karen called the room to order and made a brief introductory speech welcoming everyone, and introducing the sponsor. Bald head sweating, he stepped forward.

'You all know me for what I am,' he announced, 'or most of you will. Jim Buckley, to them as don't, Buck for short. I'm here today to present a cheque to Miss Stannard, as head of the Department of Museums and Antiquities. It's a kind of bribe, if you like, to make sure she stays off any building sites of mine, because archaeologists can cause the most bloody awful delays to building sites if they say there's something to be found there . . .'

The drumming outside seemed to be getting louder. Arnold, standing near the window, looked out. There was a scurrying of policemen, moving northward through the market area, and at the rear he caught a glimpse of a man he knew: Detective Chief Inspector Culpeper . . .

* * *

Sweating, niggled, Culpeper muttered obscenities under his breath, wondering what the hell he was supposed to be contributing, coming here to this bloody demonstration. He had made the point, in his protestations to the Assistant Chief Constable.

'I don't know that it makes sense, sir. I'm up to my eyes in a murder investigation, and you expect me to waste my time by taking up station at Alnwick—'

'The order says all available manpower,' the Assistant Chief Constable interrupted crisply. 'So that includes you.'

'But Farnsby could be spared while I get on—'

'Farnsby is excused. His presence is not necessary, and can be spared, while he carries on with the incident team.'

'But if he can be excused—'

'He's different. I want you involved as a spotter, Culpeper. You've been around a long time — you keep telling us that. You know a lot of names, people, faces. You'll be of assistance, identifying known troublemakers, picking out the rabble-rousers.'

'But there'll be cameras, sir!'

'The human eye is better,' the Assistant Chief Constable retorted primly. 'And your experienced eye will be there.'

Which it was.

But it had all been pretty boring and uneventful so far. There had been one early incident: some demonstrators had managed to sneak into the market square and had upended one of the makeshift stalls that were probably not licensed to be there anyway. Culpeper had recognized one of the stallholders involved in the brief battle: it was the man the police cadets had dubbed the Wolf Man. He was hustled away by two constables, protesting, while a demonstrator was also frogmarched away. After that, things seemed to settle down, the market was busy, the punters maybe a little edgy and nervous. There were no other illegal immigrants noticeable by their presence, the stallholders' cries were strident and confident enough, and Culpeper had even had time to sneak off to a bar at the back of one of the pubs to have a quick pint.

He'd found a quiet corner, sipped his beer, and contemplated the progress of the investigation into the death of Alex Isaacson. He wasn't getting very far. He'd hauled Sid Larson in for a good browbeating, but the man had been sullenly adamant. He had an alibi, he had not been in the pub with Isaacson whatever the barman might be saying, and he had nothing to do with the murder. Culpeper had told Farnsby to interview the barman again. They'd managed to dig a bit more into Hall Gabriel's past, and there were rumours that there might have been some skulduggery in the way he got started, how he got rid of his partner Angell, but they were rumours only and it was all a bit sketchy. And as for Professor Saul Davidson and Daniel Gibbs's father, the story of the major's dismissal from the army, there was still some real link yet to be found. But Davidson had reluctantly given up the manuscript account from the university archives, after first denying that he even recalled its existence. It was going to provide Culpeper with bedtime reading, tonight.

But for the moment, he sighed, duty called.

He finished his pint, wandered back out into the street and realized things were hotting up. From the top of the hill near the castle, there was an ominous murmuring sound, a slow buzzing of a gathering mob proceeding down the hill. At the edge of the market Culpeper could already see a few placards emerging — SAVE OUR SOCIETY and GRUNTS GO HOME seemed to be the most popular, backed up by REMOVE ROMANIAN RAPISTS. The last placard lacked conviction, somehow; the printing was shaky, as though reflecting the general view of the reliability of Sally Armstrong's evidence. Culpeper pushed his way along the assembling cordon of policemen, who had begun to move through the market towards the presumed flashpoint at the Castlegate entrance, scanning the crowd as it thickened, looking for familiar faces. It wasn't long before he caught sight of one very familiar to him. Sid Larson was capering at the edge of the advancing crowd: red-faced, bawling slogans, inciting the crowd about him, he hadn't changed in twenty years Culpeper thought, except that he seemed to enjoy the violence even more than ever. Culpeper grabbed the arm of the nearest constable, pointed out Larson, and the policeman nodded. With two colleagues, he began to push his way through the market, heading for Larson. The man saw them coming, and struggled to lose himself among his followers.

The murmur from the hill had become a wild drumming, and a few moments later the broad mass of the crowd came streaming around through the twisting streets, cardboard placards erected high on wooden staves. It wouldn't be long, Culpeper knew, before those staves would be used as offensive weapons. It was just like the old days, he thought, as he saw the three constables struggling to reach Larson, and he was too old to be involved in this kind of nonsense.

He scanned the crowd. There was another face he recognized, and another. They were not men he could quickly put names to, but he pointed them out anyway as likely troublemakers. Policemen bored their way through the market to grab them, escort them out of harm's way. A man's features sprang to his attention, hanging back in the crowd, and Culpeper was about to point the individual out to his colleagues, when he realized the man was not a potential troublemaker, but someone from Arnold Landon's department. Culpeper had heard there was some sort of meeting these Museums and Antiquities people were having in the White Swan. He must have come out to watch the fun. They chose the most peculiar times, he muttered to himself.

It was at that point he caught a glimpse of Saul Davidson.

It was a peculiar experience for Culpeper. There was a brief, flashing image in his mind, almost one of *déjà vu*. It was a dredging from his own memory and experience, and yet at the same time it was something to do with the files he had been searching through. Another time, years ago; a much younger Saul Davidson; a riot scene, police batons, the miners' strike . . .

Davidson was standing there now, at the back of the noisy crowd, pressed up against the wall. He was not actually participating. He seemed to be there more as an observer, a scrutinizer of social mores, the detached viewer of human behaviour — the academic who stands back and watches, without taking part. But Culpeper knew he had done it before, years ago, for his face had been in the old photographs. Maybe this was the role he played. The ghost at the feast, the eerie presence who was drawn to violence, but never took part in it.

Or maybe he was the one who orchestrated it.

Watching him suspiciously, Culpeper guessed that whatever the situation in the past, right now orchestration was not what it was about. Davidson might have been caught here by chance — maybe he had been shopping in the market. Certainly, he was keeping his distance, at the edge of the crowd; in no sense was he inciting it, or taking active part in the demonstration. And yet, there was something odd about the keen interest with which he was watching what was happening. Culpeper had been sent here as a spotter, but Davidson too seemed to be looking for something — or someone. He was staring around, scrutinizing faces, and for one moment his gaze locked with Culpeper's. There was a hesitation, perhaps a hint of alarmed recognition, and then Davidson's glance slipped away again, flicking around the crowd in front of him.

Next moment Culpeper lost sight of the man as there was a violent surge, a barrier went down and a roar came from the demonstrators as a spearhead group of young men tunnelled forward through the crowd and burst into the market square, shouting, flailing and whirling their placards as battle broke out in earnest. Culpeper found himself pulled forward, as the men around him piled into the front line. Placards went flying and the staves were brandished and the drumming sound burst into a crescendo. The crowd milled about, surging here and there as it met the police presence and fists were hammering, boots flailing as men were taken in headlocks; demonstrators went down kicking, the air was split with jeering and shouting and spitting and yelling, and

Culpeper's blood was up and he piled in with the others, the younger men, and it was just the way it had been in the old days . . . just like the old days . . .

'Bit of a red mist, sir?' the grinning constable asked as he helped Culpeper, dizzy, groggy, shakily to his feet, and the battle swayed and surged thirty yards away.

* * *

In the White Swan the meeting with the representatives of the media was clearly over. The reporters had edged out of the room as the sound of the tumult outside had grown, and as Jim Buckley came to the end of his short speech he found himself addressing an almost empty room. Karen Stannard's big event had collapsed, and she was clearly furious. But she put a good face on it, thanked Buckley, and suggested they go down to the bar for a drink. He refused. It was clear he also wanted to go outside to watch the action. From the excited look in his eyes, it might have been that he even wanted to join in.

'What a bloody mess,' Karen exclaimed to Arnold.

'I guess we just hit on the wrong day,' he agreed.

She shook her head in frustration, and glared at the undistributed brochures on the table. 'We didn't even get out the publicity stuff.' The shouting outside grew suddenly louder. 'What the hell is that all about anyway?'

'Illegal immigrants. I gather there are demonstrations up and down the country today.'

'I suppose it'll be some of the people you got involved with, in that pub fight of yours.'

'It's possible. I wouldn't know.'

'Well, don't think you're getting involved again. We might as well clear up here. Give me a hand with these brochures, back to my car.'

Arnold obliged. He had had enough of violence against immigrants already, his bruises had faded but his memory had not. He helped bundle up the brochures and followed

Karen out through the back entrance of the hotel into the crowded car park at the rear of the hotel. He heard her swear.

'Some idiot's blocked me in.' She glared around for a moment. 'Never mind, I'll open up the car and we can get these papers stowed, then I'll see what the hotel can do to shift that Land-Rover blocking me in.'

Arnold piled the brochures into the boot, and slammed down the lid. 'Is that it?'

She nodded. 'I'll sort out the car business. You can get away, if you like, you're parked elsewhere, anyway.'

They turned and began to walk back to the hotel, when suddenly a group of young men burst into the car park, fighting and struggling. A posse of policemen were in hot pursuit, and caps were flying as the struggling group fanned out towards Arnold and Karen. He put out an arm to protect her but in a moment, they were both caught up in the fracas, wild-eyed thugs screaming all around them, men colliding with them, knocking them sideways in their reckless flight from arrest. Arnold was spun around, but he saw a man crash blindly into Karen and she went down with a cry of pain. A policeman shouted something, the group was splitting apart, running in different directions, and the constable leaned over Arnold, chest heaving as he panted, 'Is she all right, sir?'

'I'll see to her,' Arnold assured him, and knelt beside Karen. Her eyes were filled with fury, but her mouth was twisted with pain. 'Are you okay, Karen?'

She swore luridly, with a professional commitment. He had always guessed she would have the necessary vocabulary. He helped her to her feet. She winced. 'My bloody arm . . . and wrist. Stupid, stupid idiots! Get me back to the hotel.'

In the reception area help was immediately at hand, but she brushed aside most of the proffered ministrations. She asked Arnold to get her a brandy, and she went back into the conference room they had recently used, to sit down and recover. When Arnold returned with the drink, she had removed her jacket, rolled up the *sleeve* of her white blouse, and was inspecting her arm. It was reddened, scraped from her contact with the ground. She accepted the glass from Arnold and swallowed half of its contents in one gulp. She flexed her wrist and gasped. 'Nothing to see, but it hurts like hell!'

'A sprain?' he suggested.

'I think so.' She moved her wrist in gingerly fashion, ran a hand over her shoulder and upper arm. She shook her head. 'I'm not enjoying this.'

Arnold looked around. There were still unused and half-empty wine bottles from the meeting. He walked over and poured himself a glass of wine, returned to sit down beside Karen. 'You'd better rest a while. Are you going to be able to drive?' he asked.

She shook her head doubtfully. 'Not for a while, at least.'

'Would you like me to drive you home?'

She looked at him, frowning slightly, then shook her head. 'That wouldn't make much sense. It means you'd *have* to come back for your own car, later.'

'I could get a bus. Or a lift from someone in the department, tomorrow morning.'

A dark-suited man entered the room; slight, eager, nervous, he introduced himself as the duty manager. He enquired after her injuries, and with a certain hesitation suggested in the circumstances she might wish to stay the night at the hotel. As a guest of the hotel management, naturally. She shrugged non-committally, and he left.

She thought about the suggestion while she finished the brandy. She glanced across to the wine bottles. Arnold took the hint, and brought a glass of wine across for her. 'Thanks. I wonder whether he's right. It probably is a better idea for me to stay here tonight. My arm will be stiff as hell in the morning, but I don't think I can drive at the moment, and with all those bloody hooligans out there . . . Would you mind going after him, Arnold, and accept his offer, book me a room for the night?'

'If you're certain.'

She was certain.

It was quickly arranged. Nervously sympathetic staff arranged for a room at the front of the hotel, at no charge they assured Arnold again, since she had been injured in their car park. They offered assistance to the room. She refused it, handing her car keys to Arnold, asking him to return to her car to pick up the overnight bag in the boot. 'I always carry one, just in case of emergencies,' she explained. 'And while you're at it, pick up one of the unopened bottles from the conference room and bring it up to me, with the overnight bag.' He complied, tapping on the door of her room, with the bag in one hand and the bottle under his arm. She opened the door, grimacing in pain, then gestured him inside.

'They've beaten you to it,' she said, indicating the ice-bucketed bottle of champagne which had been rapidly placed in the room ahead of Arnold's arrival.

Arnold laughed. 'I think they'll be terrified in case you make some kind of claim against them, since you were injured on the premises.'

She managed a smile. She nodded towards the champagne bottle. 'Well, if I get enough of this stuff inside me, I guess the pain will be somewhat numbed.' She paused, uncharacteristically hesitant. 'You . . . ah . . . perhaps you'll help me out a bit?'

He uncorked the champagne with a bang. He poured two glasses, they sat down, she on the settee and he in an easy chair near the window. They sipped the whispering liquid in silence. He felt a little uneasy as she laid her head back on the chair and closed her eyes for a while. At last she sighed, took another sip of champagne and said, 'I hope you're in no hurry, Arnold. At the moment I could do with some company . . . the thought of being stuck alone in Alnwick this evening is not, in the circumstances, an exciting prospect.'

He assured her he had no plans for the evening.

She caressed her shoulder and arm gingerly. 'Okay, look, why don't you sit here and have another glass while I take a shower. The hot water might ease this ache — even if the liquor doesn't yet. I shan't be long. Then you shove off downstairs, I'll get changed and maybe we could have dinner together in the hotel.' She eyed him, with a hint of a smile. 'My expense. After all, I'm a lady in trouble.'

He noted the irony in her tone, and wondered whether the evening was going to be awkward. In fact, it was not. When she had showered and changed, she rang down to reception and he returned to her room. She let him in with a smile. She wore a dark blue skirt and cream blouse, and she seemed more relaxed, her hair still damp from her shower, and from the light in her eyes he suspected she had taken another glass of the champagne provided by the hotel. They decided to finish the bottle together before an early dinner, and the conversation flowed rather more easily between them. The edge in their relationship seemed to fade. They talked about professional things and personal things. She asked him about his upbringing, and his developing interest in the work he loved, and he asked her about her own background, and her own struggle to get to the top. The time slipped past pleasantly.

When they finally went down to the dining room the noise of battle outside had long since ceased. They chose well from a good menu, and though Arnold was beginning to get nervous about the amount of alcohol he had consumed, he joined her in getting rid of a good red wine. She was good company; beautiful, at ease — apart from an occasional grimace when her arm and wrist bothered her — and it was as though the many occasions when they had clashed were erased from their memories.

Arnold could not be sure at what point a subtle change came over them, and the atmosphere sharpened in a manner that unnerved him slightly, but caused his senses to swim, also. It might have been the alcohol. It might have been her suggestion that they have a nightcap after he had seen her to her room. But there seemed a sudden lightness, a hint of recklessness in the air, an acceptance that something was different this evening, a barrier had been removed, an unstated step taken forward.

He escorted her to her room, and she invited him in again. Side by side on the settee they finished what was left of the bottle Arnold had earlier brought up to her room — the champagne was long since finished. There never actually seemed a point of time when any decisions were consciously made. There were no discussions of the advisability of it, or the foolishness of it. It was as though there was an inevitability about what was going to happen, but when they kissed it was gentle, and deliberate, and progressive. She cried out a little when she slipped the blouse from her shoulders to assist the gentle exploration of his fingers, wincing again at the pain in her wrist, but the cry turned to a murmur as his mouth found her breast.

The darkness grew around them as they grew closer, hands and mouths touching, the softness of her body merging with the urgency of his. He was unaware of any inhibition, any deliberation of the consequences of what was happening for their professional relationship. There was only the moment the heightened senses, the sharpened sensations.

They moved to the bed by unspoken, mutual agreement, and lay side by side, the length of her body against his. They undressed each other almost casually exploring. She twisted against him on the bed, moved above him. Firmly, he pushed her back, and down.

'No, like this,' he said.

'*Dominatrix dorninatus*,' she murmured, giggling. 'Or should it be *dominata*?'

'I never did Latin.'

'Mine's a bit rusty and that little phrase might be wrong,' she replied, and groaned slightly as she felt him enter her. 'At the boarding school we girls . . . used to have . . . a dirty Latin joke . . . about this . . . *Facio* . . . *facis*—'

'You're not at school now,' he interrupted and the muscles of his thighs tightened, and she gasped and then there were only murmurings that were meaningless, rhythmic, seemingly endless, drifting into the far corners of the darkened room.

* * *

Some hours later, finally, Detective Chief Inspector Culpeper put aside the manuscript written by Major Henry Gibbs. He found it difficult to sleep thereafter; the horrors depicted by the major stayed with him, and he was beginning to understand how such experiences could make a man hate with the kind of ferocity that had driven the major to found the Sons of England.

Culpeper had drifted off for only a few hours when the bedside telephone rang. Dragging himself out of what felt like a drugged sleep, he was not pleased to realize it was Farnsby on the line.

'What the hell do you want?' he growled.

Farnsby's tone was firm. 'We've got some interesting information, sir. Came in late last evening. I've just picked it up. This man Hall Gabriel, you'll recall he was in partnership with a man called Angell. Well, sir, it seems Angell had a daughter. And she got married—'

The heavy-bodied woman at Culpeper's side stirred irritably. She'd play hell with him for being woken this time in the morning. Culpeper didn't want to hear about marriage.

'Farnsby, for God's sake! Surely this can wait?'

'Ordinarily, yes, sir, but we've just had a call,' Farnsby responded crisply. 'Someone's tried to break into Abbey Manor. Gabriel himself rang in — Sean Corman's gone out after the intruder and Gabriel reckons there's been mayhem out near the stables.'

Culpeper groaned.

So did Mrs Culpeper, at his side.

Culpeper slid out of bed, and began unbuttoning his striped pyjamas. Farnsby, or someone, was going to pay for this.

3

Arnold left before dawn. Karen was still sleeping, nursing her bruised arm and wrist. His head felt thick and muzzy, and his emotions were confused.

He walked up through the darkened town. A few cars passed him, headlights blazing, people off to work outside Alnwick. The ginnel was narrow, littered with the detritus of yesterday afternoon's demonstration. He made his way to his car, unlocked it, slid behind the wheel. Then he sat there for a long time, as the slow red fingers of dawn touched the roofs of Alnwick below him.

The lovemaking had been strenuous, and there was still alcohol in his blood. He felt it unwise to face Karen imme-diately that morning. Better to steal away, give each of them time to consider what had happened between them, find some way to deal with it, and determine how it might affect their relationship in the office. Blurred thoughts of Portia Tyrrel crept unbidden into his mind, a fading memory of the brief time they had spent together on the grassy fell some months ago, and he shook his head, uncertain.

Portia had made love with him to resolve professional and emotional problems between her and Karen — but what had motivated Karen, after all these years?

He guessed Karen would go into the office today, unless her wrist and arm were too stiff. But right at this moment he didn't think he knew quite how to face her. He started the car, engaged the gears, and drove slowly down to Bondgate, and out of the town, aimlessly.

His mind was on automatic as far as driving was concerned. His thoughts surged with images of the woman he had been with, the softness of her skin, the firmness of her breasts, and the way they had writhed together, locked in a passion that was not easily spent. He had wondered for years what it might be like, to make love with Karen Stannard — now he knew, and yet the memory was hazy and blurred, a combination of alcohol and passion, touch and sensation. The car breasted the slope of the hill and the sun, rising low in the sky, was suddenly bright in his eyes. He slowed, pulled into the side of the narrow road, and shook his head, pulling himself together in the wandering confusion of his mind. He looked about him, considered where he was.

In the distance, glittering in the early morning sunlight, was the bright, beaten gold expanse of the sea. He had driven north, away from Alnwick, perhaps almost unconsciously steering away from Morpeth and the office. Inland were the towering shoulders of the Cheviot, dark, almost menacing against the fading intensity of the early morning sky.

He was on the road to Abbey. It was understandable, really. He had been driving there so regularly for the last few weeks, his mental automatic pilot had brought him here now. And it was a good enough place to go, to think things through, to dwell on what had happened last night, and the possible consequences. There would be no one there from the department. The sea cave had been placed out of bounds since the discovery of the body of Alex Isaacson in the vulvic depths of Hades Gate. Their work had been disturbed first by the bones of a twenty-year-old death, and now by the killing of a young man. Perhaps the evil reputation of the rock fissure was well earned. Perhaps the sea cave had always held such secrets and such dangers.

Arnold drove slowly onwards towards Abbey Head as the red dawn changed to a blue, cloud-bruised sky.

There was no reason to go down the track to the sea cave itself. He parked the car in the shadow of the ruined abbey, and sat there, gazing out to sea. He wondered briefly when the police would allow them to go back to the cave, but then his thoughts returned to Karen, unbidden. He remembered the way it had been between them, and his body moved. Unsettled, he got out of the car, stepped around towards the clifftop, and suddenly realized he was not alone on the headland.

He heard a vague shouting, and looked about him. He was partly screened from the road and the track down to the beach by the stark ruined walls of the ancient abbey itself, but across the headland, running towards him from the spinney that darkened the horizon above Abbey Manor, sited on the slope to the right, were two men.

He could make out little detail at first. One was stocky, and seemed to be staggering somewhat, his running mazy and undirected. Some fifty yards behind him was a second man, taller, leaner, and it was he who was shouting in pursuit.

Arnold hesitated. It was none of his business and he had no idea what was going on but the man in front seemed to be staggering more than ever, and slowly Arnold began to walk forward, on a line which would cross their progress. Then he saw the man in front fall to his knees, stay there with his head down, chest heaving. The taller man caught up with him and stood above him, hands on his thighs, bowed forward, trying to catch his breath as he harangued the man crouched on the turf at his feet. He put out a hand, half lifted him to his feet, but there was a shouted curse, the pursued man threw off the assistance and began to walk away again, lurching slightly.

It was only then that Arnold recognized the shorter, stocky man. With a sense of shock, he shouted, 'Hayman! Chris Hayman!'

Both men stopped, looked in his direction, and now Arnold recognized the tall, slightly stooping figure of the pursuer also: it was Professor Saul Davidson, dressed in dark, high-necked sweater, jeans and boots. He stared at Arnold for several seconds, then swung away, starting to argue furiously with Hayman, who again thrust his restraining hand away and broke into a half run, in the direction of the cliff edge.

And Arnold realized that between Hayman and the cliff edge was the yawning maw of Hades Gate.

Arnold began to run, waving his arms and calling out at the top of his voice. Both men ignored him. Davidson was long-legged, quicker than Hayman and he caught up with him some thirty feet from the edge of the rock fissure. As he pounded up, Arnold could hear Davidson shouting angrily, insistently, but the words were tossed away, meaningless in the headland breeze. But as he grew closer Arnold could make out the dark stain of blood oozing from Hayman's matted scalp, marking his wild-eyed features, glistening in the morning sunshine.

The two men were locked together, struggling. As Arnold arrived near them he reached out, grabbed at Davidson's shoulder, and the man turned, his face suffused with anger, glaring at Arnold in fury. 'He's been up at Abbey Manor! He's half beaten Sean Corman to death!'

Chris Hayman was like a man possessed with devils. He broke free of Davidson's arms and pushed. Caught off balance Davidson lurched into Arnold, then fell sideways with a cry of pain. He lay on the grass, panting, staring up at Hayman. Arnold put out a hand. 'Chris — what's this about, for God's sake?'

'Stay out of this,' Hayman muttered. 'Stay away from me. And keep that dog of hell at a distance.'

Uncomprehending, Arnold glanced at Saul Davidson, still lying on the grass, his ankle twisted under him. Grimacing with pain, Davidson pleaded, 'Hayman, don't make things worse for yourself. Gabriel will have phoned . . . the police will be coming. Calm down, think things through, we can work all this out yet!'

'Work things out!' The words came out viciously, spitting with anger. Hayman stepped forward and before Arnold could stop him he launched a kick at Davidson's chest. The professor rolled, taking most of the force from the blow, but he cried out in pain again as his ankle was jarred further. Arnold stepped forward, grabbing at Hayman. 'For God's sake, calm down! What the hell's going on here?'

Hayman twisted free, a low sob in his throat as he stared at Arnold. It was as though he was recognizing him for the first time. But he backed away, limping slightly, brushing the blood from his eyes as it trickled from the wound in his hairline. Arnold could see now that Hayman had taken a bad beating . . . But Davidson had said Corman was in a worse condition.

'Chris, tell me, what's happening?'

Hayman ignored him, but began to walk backwards towards the looming gap in the rock behind him. Arnold kept his tone even, though the blood was pounding in his head. 'Chris, be careful. The fissure is right behind you.'

'Hades Gate,' Hayman hissed.

'Don't go back any further!'

Hayman was standing on the edge of the fissure now.

His face was pale, dark-blood streaks giving him an almost satanic appearance. In the distance, beyond Abbey Manor, Arnold heard the sound of vehicles. A few moments later he caught sight of two police cars edging across on to the headland. Hayman saw them, watched them dully, careless. Arnold put out a hand. 'Come on, Chris, let's get away from this.'

Hayman's eyes were glazed. He took a deep, shuddering breath. Behind Arnold the cars came to a halt, tyres screeching. Arnold heard a voice he knew. Culpeper.

'All right, Mr Landon, leave it to us now. Just quietly back away.'

Culpeper's tone was authoritative. Arnold moved to comply, but in that moment Chris Hayman stepped backwards and his foot slipped in the damp long grass fringing the edge of the fissure. He lurched, began to slide backwards and Arnold threw himself towards him, scrabbling to his knees to

183

reach for him. Then he was lying on the edge of the fissure, grabbing at the sleeve of Hayman's dark windcheater as the man slid inexorably into the gaping chasm.

For a moment Hayman scrabbled with his feet, panic-stricken, and then he looked back behind Arnold at the policemen running forward. Something changed in his eyes, a dawning realization, an acceptance of reality and he was still, bracing himself against the bubbled rock Arnold's fingers dug into the sleeve, desperately trying to hang on, but Hayman was staring at him, eyes wild.

'It was all that bastard Gabriel's doing,' he said in a harsh, unforgiving tone.

Yet as Hayman dragged and pulled deliberately at Arnold's fingers, twisted out of his grasp and fell backwards into the darkness of Hades Gate, Arnold had the thought that the unforgiving tone was in reality directed at Chris Hayman himself.

4

The Assistant Chief Constable leaned back in his chair, placed his stubby fingers on the desk in front of him, and frowned. His eyes flicked from Farnsby to Culpeper and back again.

'So your early thoughts that Sid Larson was involved in all this were erroneous,' he suggested in a reedy, supercilious tone.

Culpeper shrugged. 'He was involved twenty years ago, in as much as he took part in the organized riots then, as he was involved last Wednesday in the punch-up at Alnwick. But, no, he was just one of a number of pawns. Gun fodder on the periphery. Most of them former members of a defunct nationalist organization called the Sons of England.'

'What part did Saul Davidson play?'

'The orchestrator,' Culpeper nodded. 'Not of the Alnwick demonstration, of course, because he got out of it all, twenty years ago, but I saw him there. He was looking for Chris Hayman. He knew the man was unstable, had been since his wife committed suicide. He wanted to talk to Hayman, was trying to head him off. Stop everything coming out.'

The Assistant Chief Constable nodded thoughtfully. 'So tell me all about it. The Chief is already on my back.' Culpeper took a deep breath. He glanced at Farnsby.

They had interviewed Saul Davidson together.

The man had been broken. Recent events had dragged back into his life an episode he had almost forgotten, although it must have been buried just beneath the surface of his consciousness, a hidden guilt. He had not been entirely truthful with Culpeper earlier. He had not fully explained the disgust he had felt, the need to leave Mossad when he had guessed what had happened. And meeting Hayman at the sea cave one day had brought it all back, that and the arrival of Alex Isaacson. He had tried to contain it thereafter, prevent the inexorable, inevitable march of events, but they had all conspired to bring about the result he had dreaded.

'It all started twenty years ago, and more, when Saul Davidson took up his position as a lecturer at Newcastle,' Culpeper explained. 'He's admitted he'd been recruited by Mossad, as a sleeper, a provider of information, and he insists now that the Winder thing was the only active matter he ever really got involved in. Anyway, it was he who started the rumours about Arthur Winder's true identity, and the newspapers picked it up, but the miners' strike and other unrest, it sort of pushed the Winder issue to the back page. That didn't suit Davidson's handlers. They pressurized him to take further action.'

'This is where this man Hayman comes in?'

Culpeper nodded affirmation. 'Chris Hayman was a student in Davidson's department. It's not entirely clear how active he was in student demonstrations — though there is one file I came across where I saw his face in the front line.' He shot a triumphant glance in Farnsby's direction, but the inspector stared straight ahead. 'However, he was certainly active enough for Davidson to use him for his own purposes. Because Hayman's mother was from Poland, he even spoke a little Polish. More important, he hated the Nazis because of what had happened to his family in the concentration camps.

And he was a member of an organization called the Sons of England. Saul Davidson told him about Otto Wenschoff, explained that the man had entered England and was masquerading under the name of Arthur Winder.' He hesitated. 'Davidson seems to have deliberately targeted the membership of Sons of England — and picked up other recruits in his smear campaign against Winder. Sid Larson included.'

The Assistant Chief Constable scratched at his ear. 'But this young man — Isaacson — he was of the opinion that Wenschoff was a man of some humanity. Not a killer.'

Culpeper shrugged. 'Maybe, maybe not. Who can tell, after all this time? Anyway, twenty years ago, backed by information from Mossad, Davidson persuaded Hayman of Winder's guilt, and took steps to get the Sons of England involved in the campaign. It was a fateful decision, because it brought in Major Henry Gibbs.'

'The owner of Abbey Manor.'

Culpeper nodded. 'And the actual founder of Sons of England. Also, because of his experiences in the war, a rabid opponent of East Europeans generally. With a huge sense of injustice, because he felt he'd been badly treated in the army, by a court martial. Gibbs was only too happy to assist — he was introduced to Davidson by Chris Hayman, and that's probably where the wheel came off the wagon.'

'How do you mean?'

'Things spun out of control. Davidson had started it all, up to that point thought he was in charge of operations, but suddenly, as the press coverage was actually dying down, Winder disappeared.' Culpeper lowered his head, considered his notes.

'In our discussions with Davidson,' Farnsby offered, 'he still denied vehemently that he had anything to do with the disappearance of Arthur Winder. He admits that at the time he felt a certain relief when Winder vanished, because Davidson was already losing faith in what he was being asked to do. He saw himself as an academic, not a manhunter. So, he says, he was relieved, washed his hands of the whole business — and never enquired just what might have happened to the ex-Auschwitz camp guard.'

The Assistant Chief Constable's eyes narrowed. 'But he must have had suspicions, surely.'

'That's it precisely, sir,' Culpeper went on. 'He knew damned well that in getting the Sons of England involved he'd unleashed forces he had no control over. Major Gibbs was fanatical in his hatred. I'm pretty certain that Davidson guessed that Chris Hayman, acting in concert with and under the leadership of Major Gibbs, had taken matters into their own hands, kidnapped Winder, murdered — *executed* him in their terminology, and disposed of the body. We know now that they bundled him into Hades Gate.'

'Davidson had no way of knowing that, of course,' Farnsby suggested.

'But he didn't make any enquiries either, in spite of any suspicions he might have had. And after that, all was quiet. Winder had gone. Davidson was left with an uneasy feeling, suspicious, guilty. So he took the easy way out, simply walked away from it all. He resigned from Mossad, had no more dealings with the Sons of England. Chris Hayman struggled on at the university for a while, but eventually dropped out and took a job in the Department of Museums and Antiquities at Morpeth. And lost touch with Davidson.'

'And it all faded into the past,' Farnsby added. 'Particularly when Major Gibbs shot himself, and the Sons of England disbanded.'

'Until years later, when Alex Isaacson turned up, probing into what had happened to Arthur Winder.'

The Assistant Chief Constable frowned. 'So it seems Hayman also killed Isaacson? But why would he do that? Winder was dead and buried — there was no clear contact or link between Hayman and Winder. Major Gibbs had killed himself years before. Davidson was keeping his head down — and his mouth shut. How did Hayman even come into contact with Isaacson?'

Culpeper sighed. 'An unhappy series of coincidences, it seems. First, the fact that Hall Gabriel bought Abbey Manor.'

'What the hell's that got to do with anything?'

'In itself, nothing. But it coincided with, first, the arrival of Alex Isaacson, searching for Winder, and second, with the death of Chris Hayman's wife. Suicide.'

'How did Mrs Hayman's death affect issues?'

Culpeper shook his head sadly. 'We've pieced it together now, from what we've learned of Gabriel's background, and Hayman's wife. Before she married, she was called Sylvie Angell — and her father was in business with Hall Gabriel. But it seems Gabriel encouraged Angell's drinking and gambling habits, and, well, if he didn't exactly cheat him, at least he took advantage of him when he bought him out. Angell went into decline, and died. Hayman had married Angell's daughter — and Sylvie Angell never let her husband forget how things could have been. She became withdrawn; they lived in a tight, self-enclosed world. And when depression eventually got the better of her, she killed herself — just as Hall Gabriel wealthy, arrogant, successful, came back to buy Abbey Manor and lord it around the locality.'

'It was too much for Hayman, sir,' Farnsby offered. 'He snapped. He wanted revenge on Gabriel for what he saw as the ruination of his life and his wife's. A bit irrational, maybe, but—'

'He started prowling around Abbey Manor at night,' Culpeper cut in. 'Gabriel complained to me about it. Hayman sneaked in and damaged his cars. And he went up there after watching the demonstration in Alnwick. Sean Corman caught him sneaking around — but Hayman was stronger than he thought. Corman came off worse, Gabriel heard the shouting and phoned for the police. That's how we came to be there, on the headland.'

'It doesn't explain how Davidson came to be there,' the Assistant Chief Constable demurred.

Culpeper shrugged. 'Ever since Isaacson went missing, Saul Davidson's been worried. When he was at the sea cave he saw Hayman, and recognized him from years back. He was concerned — his old training wasn't a complete waste of time. He'd long ago guessed that Major Gibbs and Hayman had done away with Winder, and now he discovered that Hayman was sneaking around Abbey Manor. The man was behaving strangely. Davidson didn't know about the reasons for Hayman's hatred of Gabriel but he was concerned about the thought of Isaacson and Hayman meeting. He knew such a meeting could be explosive. And when Isaacson disappeared he put two and two together: Hayman hanging around Abbey Manor, Isaacson going up there, and disappearing.'

'Do we now know what exactly happened?'

'Davidson wanted to find out for certain. He had been looking for Hayman. He wanted it out with him, to find out if he had been crazy enough to kill Isaacson. That's why he was up at Abbey Manor the other night: he'd gone looking for Hayman, saw the fight between Sean Corman and Hayman, and then was screaming at Hayman to pull himself together, tell the truth, sort out his mind. But by then, Hayman was too far gone . . .'

'This man Landon?' the Assistant Chief Constable queried.

'God knows why he was there,' Culpeper muttered. 'Innocent bystander, it seems. He tried to save Hayman, but the man didn't want saving. It had all become too much for him, and with Davidson screaming at him about Isaacson . . .'

'But why did Hayman kill the young man?'

Culpeper frowned. 'Hayman had been skulking around Abbey Manor. We think he saw Isaacson visit Gabriel, and became curious. Anything to do with Gabriel obsessed Hayman. He followed Isaacson to the pub, joined him there for a drink. And then Isaacson told him about his quest, gave him his views about Arthur Winder — how he had been a good man — how he was searching for him, the man who had saved his family.'

'You can imagine the effect that would have on Hayman, sir,' Farnsby opined. 'Under Major Gibbs's leadership, he had murdered Arthur Winder all those years ago. Now, Isaacson was undermining that action, calling it into question. At the time, Hayman and Gibbs, they had acted in the belief they were serving justice in feeding their own hatred. Now, Isaacson was questioning that belief. Hayman snapped, violently disagreed. Or maybe it was just that he couldn't handle the spectre of his actions twenty years ago looming up in front of him; the thought that it might all have been wrong. Or maybe it was spur of the moment — we'll never know. It could even have been with a malicious irony that Hayman took Isaacson to Hades Gate, to show him where Winder had died. And then, pushed Isaacson in as well.'

There was a long, reflective silence. The Assistant Chief Constable grunted unhappily. 'Well, there's not much we can do about Davidson, if he's denying everything as far as his involvement in recent events is concerned. But I still have one little niggle — I hope there's nothing happened to suggest that we should have cleared all this up earlier, before this man Corman got beaten, before Hayman himself took the jump.' He glared at Culpeper. 'Is there anything?'

Culpeper was silent. Farnsby moistened lips that were suddenly dry. 'I think I have to say, sir, that there was one thing . . . I wasn't sufficiently precise. When I interviewed the barman at the Black Horse in Abbey village, he told me the man he had seen with Isaacson on the evening he died was the man who started the fight with the immigrants, earlier. I assumed he meant Sid Larson.' He flickered a nervous glance towards Culpeper. 'But of course, it wasn't Larson who actually started the fight that day: we learn now from Mr Landon that it was actually Chris Hayman. He couldn't stand the presence of Romanians in the bar, it brought out his buried racism. It was Hayman started the fight — but I missed that.'

Good lad, Culpeper thought to himself. Playing it straight for once.

'It was an easy enough mistake to make,' he suggested amiably, 'And I don't think finally we could have prevented what happened.'

The Assistant Chief Constable clucked his tongue. 'All right. But . . . this Major Gibbs, he was an ex-army man, disciplined one imagines, what on earth changed him, to set up this mob the Sons of England, and finally, to commit murder twenty years ago?'

Culpeper shuffled his feet. 'I've read some of his personal papers, sir. He was thinking of writing a book. His son placed it in the university library after his father shot himself. Self-loathing is my guess. But the book . . . I think there are answers there.'

'Hmmm. Well, it's all a long time ago.' The Assistant Chief Constable drummed his fingers on the desk again. 'All right . . . At least we made a good showing at Alnwick. Many arrests?'

'Quite a few. Including Sid Larson.'

The senior officer's eyes misted with the happy thought. 'Good . . . but you know, I wonder . . . do you think that the Auschwitz guard Otto Wenschoff really was Arthur Winder? I mean, there's never been any hard proof, has there?'

Culpeper straightened, kept his tone innocent and amiable. 'I'd be happy to try to find out, sir, if you think it demands a degree of priority.'

He was rewarded by a deep, glowering silence.

THE END